THE MIDLIFE CRISIS OF A
PERFECT
WOMAN

BELA GARY

Published by Mindstir Media, LLC
45 Lafayette Rd | Suite 181| North Hampton, NH 03862 | USA
1.800.767.0531 | www.mindstirmedia.com

Printed in the United States of America

ISBN: 978-1-7358186-0-3

DEDICATION

To my father, John Briscoe. I know you are watching over us, smiling, proud, and sometimes shaking your head. You are missed every day. I would not be where I am now, at this moment in time, without your wisdom and love.

ACKNOWLEDGEMENTS

Many, many thanks to all of you who supported me on this journey. To my children, who completely transformed my life and gave me a deep appreciation of what it means to love unconditionally. Even when I thought I would never finish this book, you never doubted. I love you both. Thank you also to the rest of my zany and supportive family for always providing love, laughter, and adventure. Thanks to my patient friends, who tirelessly listened to my stories and believed I was not insane. To the team at Seacoast Press, thank you for everything, especially for a book cover design that moved me to tears. Finally, thank you to the Universe for teaching me what it means to grow as you live, as well as for helping me see the beauty in everything. Every breath is a new experience, and every day a new adventure.

The Midlife Crisis of a Perfect Woman

True love is eternal, infinite, and always like itself.
~ Honoré de Balzac

I will keep on loving you until eternity comes
to make me love you more.
~ Munia Khan

Love is energy: it can neither be created nor destroyed. It just is
and always will be, giving meaning to life and direction to goodness.
Love will never die.
~ Bryce Courtenay

When you vibrate at the frequency of love, nothing can hurt
you. The whole universe will surrender!
~ Eckhart Tolle

An Awakening

Who looks outside, dreams. Who looks inside, awakens.
~ Carl Jung

All the powers in the universe are already ours. It is we who
have put our hands before our eyes and cry that it is dark.
~ Swami Vivekananda

An awakening can happen in a flash.
And in a flash, you are changed forever.
~ Phil Good

Even loss and betrayal can bring us an awakening.
~ Gautama Buddha

Some stories need to be told, either as a catharsis or simply as a profound story of a journey. My story serves both those purposes. Everyone has a story. How did you end up where you are right now, at this precise moment in time? Every experience in your life continually forms the person you are and the person you will become. Stop and examine who you are—you can clearly see how the good and bad have shaped you into a unique being.

I've been on a quest my entire life to find meaning. Since childhood, I was fascinated with life after death, extraterrestrial life forms, God... but without a real belief in those things, they were just a curiosity. I found them fascinating and wondered how they all tied into my own existence. I used to feel a sense of not belonging. Many of us feel out of place at times, even if we don't openly admit it. There is more to who we are as humans than just ego and material desires. We hunger to find a deeper meaning. Why are we all connected? And how? Why am I here? What is *my* purpose? These thoughts pushed me to find answers, because I knew there had to be something more beyond my everyday existence. Then I fell asleep for many years. I stopped wondering.

A series of events eventually awakened me and forced me to confront the questions I had ignored for many years. There had always been a longing in me for meaning, something profound and magical. I felt lost, until I took a huge leap of faith that completely transformed my life. I finally discovered the meaning behind that longing.

Some of the choices I made along the way were difficult and often created confusion. At times, I questioned whether I had taken a wrong turn, but I kept moving forward. I knew that I was being guided down a path that I needed to follow. This gave me freedom and the ability to think and act independently, something I realized I had never done in my life. I was always moving from relationship to relationship (always long term) but never experiencing what it's like to truly be on my own. To quote the overused cliché, I needed to find myself. And I did. And more. There is so much more that I am connected to, *we all* are connected to, that is far deeper than ever imagined in our everyday lives.

This is a story of a transformational journey and a rebirth, a blending of fact and fiction. Parts of it may seem unbelievable. It is your choice as the reader to decide what you believe.

As for me, I believe in everything.

And to think I almost didn't take that leap of faith. I didn't want to, but I was inexplicably pulled forward. Sometimes you just have to follow your intuition.

I

THE BEGINNING OF EVERYTHING

ADAM & EVE

To get the full value of joy
You must have someone to divide it with.
After all these years I see that I was mistaken about Eve
in the beginning; it is better to live outside the Garden
with her than inside it without her.
~ Mark Twain

The feeling is so overwhelming,
Making me drown in the sea of love
Where there is only you and me,
Just like the days of Adam and Eve.
~ Unknown

In the beginning, the Divine proclaimed, let there be light. The light shone throughout the universe, igniting atoms and molecules, filling the empty space with energy and matter. Stars burst forth, supernovae, galaxies, solar systems, and planets. An infinite amount, there was no time, no distance. All was one. One supreme being of energy that multiplied and evolved, over what we would consider billions of years, but which was, in reality, no time at all. There was no concept of time. All is instantaneous and all is eternal. Soon there were many points of light, each unique yet part of the collective that formed the universe.

They both were suddenly awakened into existence. They were just *there* and they didn't question where they came from nor where they were going or why they existed. They just were. They lived in the moment and the universe was their paradise. They did not know each other. Adam, quiet and mostly thoughtful, observed his surroundings. The place was peaceful, beautiful, and safe. He didn't want for anything. But a feeling grew in him that something was missing. Something was not quite right. He felt a longing. He felt incomplete. He discovered loneliness, although he could not explain it in words. He desired something, but he didn't know what. So he set out in search of an answer.

Eve burst into existence with her soul wide open, fearless. She lived in the moment, until the day she also felt a longing. There was no concept of what it could be in her mind, because all she knew was the here and now. She imagined she was unique and alone, and although she was content with that for most of her existence, she too began to ache for something indescribable. She ventured out in search of her own answers.

They were beams of light, moving in all directions at once until they zig-zagged into each other. In that instance, they sensed that they had known each other eternally. It was a sudden recognition, a familiarity, a connectedness. Because they were both part of the light, it was a knowing.

Eve whispered to Adam, "I am home."

Adam stretched his fingers, light emanating towards her from his fingertips. "My soul is yours and yours is mine. Our two halves create the whole."

Eve smiled.

The longing was gone.

They were happy, serene, like most light beings. But there was a change coming. A different kind of energy, born of a random interaction between light and matter, made its way into the universe. There were many vivid colors of light in their world, but this one was different. It was colorless, and it was clear, and so very bright. They both sensed it. Adam and Eve were fascinated by its novelty and intrigued by its ambiguity. They were curious and recognized its uniqueness. They allowed the light to merge with them. Instantly, they became aware of things that were once forbidden. Instead of just being, they saw the future, they knew the past, they sensed time, they recognized evil. They felt sadness, although they did not know what it meant. They felt and wondered.

Their world shifted again and they were suddenly earthbound creatures, on a physical plane, no longer immersed in many dimensions at once; they were solidly in one dimension. Limited. No longer free. However, there was freedom, because they now had free will. They could not just *be* anymore. They sensed a future and felt a pull to move forward toward it. They wondered about their past. They were aware. At the same time, their minds and memories became clouded, foggy. They weren't exactly sure where they had come from and how they had come into being.

They saw themselves as matter—solid, not just light beings an in infinite state. The solidity confused them. They had a beginning and an end, and they could not go beyond their physical bodies and reach out to the light of the universe. They were limited instead of limitless, finite instead of infinite. Adam tried to tell Eve what he was experiencing, but his mind was no longer connected with hers, so the thought stayed stuck in his own consciousness. Eve, fearful, was at that same moment trying to connect to Adam. Finding that she could not make contact, she responded by sending out her energy. In that moment, her mouth opened, and she let out a primal scream. Both Adam and Eve were surprised by the sound. They had never heard a sound before. Eve opened her mouth again and let out a soft "ah" sound. She released more sounds, practicing her newly discovered ability. Adam did the same and was amazed.

"Eve...Eve...Eve," he stuttered.

She whispered back to him, "Adam."

They looked at each other's bodies, touched them. They were nearly the same but noticed the differences. They explored their bodies, feeling the softness of the skin, the texture of the hair. Adam reached over to Eve's breast. Eve shuddered. At that first touch, they both felt the deep, immediate connectedness, like they had known each other since the beginning and would know each other into the infinite future. They loved each other. They did not name the feeling, but instantly they knew that they were one. They felt like this was where they should be. They were home.

They discovered each other's bodies, discovered sexual pleasure, the ecstasy of orgasm. It was all trial and error, although part of them knew exactly what they could do to please the other. While they were still connected at a certain level, they lost the concept of being one whole. They did nothing but spend time together and enjoy the pleasure of their bodies and touch, the pleasantness of spoken words, how the loving words gave them joy and warmth. Hunger soon became known to them, and they noticed the passage of time. Adam and Eve followed their instincts, ate from the garden, and soon learned how to survive as mortals.

However, this earthly awakening and their newfound knowledge also came with a price. They found they could only understand each other and communicate if the other allowed it. They no longer could read each other's minds and know everything the other was thinking. And they found that they did not have to tell the truth. They could say whatever the other wanted to hear. So came the first lie and betrayal.

Eve was on her own one day close to the boundary they had never crossed. Out of the corner of her eye, she saw movement. She turned and on the ground was an animal she had never seen before. It was long and moved along the ground. She was curious and walked over. Immediately, she sensed an energy she hadn't felt before. It was not pure light. It was the opposite of light. She moved closer until she was able to touch the creature. She reached out, gently brushed her hand on its back, and immediately pulled away. There was pain, searing pain that was not only physical, but which touched her heart in such a way that she instantly felt sorrow. She turned and ran back to tell Adam what had happened. As she ran, the darkness crept further into her soul.

"Eve, what's wrong?" questioned Adam, bewildered and concerned.

"I'm not sure..." She stared at Adam and answered as if in a daze. "Nothing."

She touched her hand to her heart and looked him in the eye. "I just ate a bad berry."

Adam was confused, because he felt that it was something more.

"Eve, I don't understand...you are different." He reached for her hand.

The instant he touched her, the pain grew, and she was filled with fear. She did not want him to touch her. It was not right, it was wrong; there was something terribly wrong.

"*No!* Adam, please!" she screamed. "I don't feel well."

She ran away from him, panicked by what was happening to her, ashamed because she had yelled at Adam. Eve was usually so open and never hid anything from him, and she had never spoken so angrily before.

What Adam couldn't see nor understand was that she was no longer as innocent as he and that being with him now was more difficult and complicated. She felt sadness, pain, and rage being near him, and when he touched her, those feelings exploded inside of her like many tiny sharp blades. She did not tell him the truth because she was afraid. *But why am I afraid?* She couldn't understand the sudden fear inside her, the darkness that seemed to continue growing.

Perhaps if she had been honest with him, things might have turned out differently. She knew no other way out except to hide everything from Adam.

Eve's encounter and subsequent lie led to fear and mistrust. Adam no longer believed the words she spoke. His anger over her betrayal festered, until it overtook the love he once felt for her. Eve continued to separate herself from him, widening the gap in their connection, until finally, both of their hearts were filled with sorrow. Life went on for them, and humanity as we know it now continued forward. Adam and Eve never were able to reconnect spiritually again. They were together only in physical form, out of necessity and loneliness, but their soul was permanently split in two. They were never able to unite as one again in their lifetime.

THE BLUE ISLAND

Ever feel like you don't belong on earth?
~ Binnt Hassan

What we don't know is much more than what we know.
~ Albert Einstein

Sehnsucht:
(n.) the inconsolable longing in the human heart for we know not what;
a yearning for a far, familiar, non-earthly land one can identify
as one's home

She was born on a tiny Portuguese island on a chilly and windy fall afternoon. The weather was always unpredictable at this time of the year. This day was cold and stormy, with out-of-control waves crashing over the sea wall. It was an uneventful birth. She clearly remembers the moment of her birth. She remembers coming into the world, a dark tunnel, and the fear of being thrust back into the physical world. The experience was not new to her—she had done this before. And then peace. The love she felt upon arrival made up for her fear of not being connected to the light or her other half. Then she forgot everything that came before her birth.

She went home the next day, just another newborn island baby. However, she was more than that. Her life had already been predetermined. The Divine knew how her life would flow and what joys and burdens lay in her path. She had made this choice before birth, a contract, an agreement with her other half. She would precede him in this lifetime on the planet by a few years, and they would not meet until many years in the future. They had lessons to learn and hopefully, in this lifetime, they would finally be together. They had known each other in countless previous lives but never reached the point of union and enlightenment.

Her early years were full of love from her mother, her grandparents, other relatives, and friends. She was the most beautiful baby on the island, according to all who saw her. Her proud grandfather would take her everywhere, boasting of the beauty of his granddaughter. Peace, tranquility, and love filled her life.

The happy times didn't last long though. Her father, who had left shortly after her birth to fight a war, returned a changed man. His return should have been a happy event, but he was consumed with darkness and hate. He suffered trauma that was never explained to her. His anger turned to abuse. She didn't have precise memories of those events—she likely effectively blocked those out. She only recalled a sense of unhappiness and fear that suddenly filled her world.

Her sister was also born on the island, just one-and-a-half years later. People would eventually think they were twins, although her sister had dark hair and skin more typical of the island natives. Her mother would often take both girls for long walks: to the park, the cemetery, anywhere, simply to get away from the darkness that was in their home. Sometimes they would walk for a long time. She knew she liked being out of that house with her mother and sister. Escape. That would be one of the themes of her life as she grew older.

A few years passed. She had a few vague memories of her childhood on the island. She remembered trying to feed clothespins to the chickens (thankfully, the chickens didn't find them appetizing). In a foggy haze, she remembered getting some sort of injection in her stomach after cutting her lip open on a metal chair. Or was that a dream? And of course, the terror caused by a close encounter with a cow. Cows would still scare her well into adulthood. *Why do painful events stick to our memory easier?*

However, her most vivid memory was of an encounter in the park with a blind, old woman, who was rumored to be a witch. The girl was in the park feeding the swans and saw the woman coming towards her, using a stick made of bamboo to feel the ground in front of her as she walked. She had heard about her from stories the other children told—how she had chased them and how she wasn't really blind, but just pretending so that she could trap the children and then take them home and imprison them. The girl was nervous. Her grandfather was on the other side of the park talking to his friends. The woman kept coming towards her, her cane click-clicking on the sidewalk.

"Little girl," the woman croaked, in a deep, manly voice. "Little girl, I know who you are."

She should have been frightened of the woman, but instead she was curious. She didn't run and waited for the woman to approach her.

"I am me," she replied confidently.

"Ah," breathed the old woman, as she placed her hand suddenly upon the girl's head. The girl was scared. *What does this witch want from me?* But she couldn't bring herself to move.

Her whole body convulsed, and she saw lights—deep, beautiful, green lights. They were swirling in front of her, the most brilliant lights she had ever seen. The colors then changed to an intense golden light. *What is happening to me?*

The light vanished. She stood on a hill, and she could hear the crash of waves on a nearby shore. She turned around and saw a tiger. His entire body quivered, his mouth opened slightly, and he bared his teeth. She froze. *Is this real? Maybe if I stand still, he will go away.* Then the tiger let out a deafening roar. In terror, she ran. He lunged after her. She ran as fast as she could, her tiny legs a blur of movement, trying to escape. Without warning, she came to a cliff and could go no farther. She stopped and closed her eyes, fearing this was the end. Then, unexpectedly, the tiger ended his chase. He looked at her and growled softly.

She was out of breath and panting. "Who are you?"

The tiger growled softly again, but this time she understood words.

"You will be running from yourself, your fears, for many years because you won't know who you truly are and you will walk the wrong path. You will fail to comprehend for a long time, until you meet a man who will change the way you look at the world. Then you will become the tiger and chase that man to a cliff, where he will finally realize what he has been running from," he rumbled softly, lying casually in front of her.

She was so confused. She felt a sudden vibration and saw a swirl of colors. The last thing she glimpsed as she was pulled away from her dream was a man. She knew him. *I have dreamed of him before!*

"Wait!" she shouted, as she saw him slowly dissolve. "Wait, who are you?"

There was no reply, as she was whisked back to the park, the old woman's hand still on her head.

"What was that? A dream?" she asked in confusion.

"Little girl. It is your future. Remember who you are and where you come from and remember this day. You will have to stop running from the tiger one day, and you will need the courage to become the tiger and give chase."

And with that, the woman removed her hand from the girl's head and went click-clicking back across the park.

She was confused, stunned, and simply stood there, unable to move or call out. Her thoughts were muddled, and she felt tears pooling in her eyes. *How can I run from myself? This doesn't make sense. And who is this man that I know but have never met?*

She took a breath and looked for her grandfather. She couldn't see him at first and felt panic. *There he is.* She ran to him and gave him a huge hug, her confusion and fear slowly dissipating. *It's time for ice cream!* He took her hand and she skipped along beside him, letting the experience slowly imbed itself in the part of her mind where all forgotten memories go.

This memory would remain in her subconscious until she was much older, and the tiger would appear again in her dreams.

As she got older, she felt a longing for something she couldn't explain. It was not something tangible. It was an emotion? She couldn't describe it with any clarity. It was something unknown, but she wanted it. She needed it. Was it just because her life was not ideal, that she wished for another life? Sometimes she wished she had been born into a different world, universe, existence; one filled with more peace and love. There was an increasing darkness surrounding her. In those moments, she remembered something she couldn't quite articulate that gave her comfort. A feeling? A memory? Something was missing. She did not feel complete. Yet, she felt she was special and unique and different. And she knew a secret that others did not. Something was going to happen. One day.

THE MYSTERIOUS CONTINENT

Faith is not believing that God can. It is knowing that God will.
~ Ben Stein

Inside every cynical person is a disappointed idealist.
~ George Carlin

The little boy was born on a hot African day. Moments after his birth, his mother handed the dark-haired baby to his father, who looked into the tiny baby's eyes and instantly loved him. He was the child of missionaries, spreading the word of God to the people of that country. He was very much loved. His parents had good hearts and a lot of love to give.

His family lived a simple life. They had some hired help, but far fewer than most of the other white ex-pats who lived in the city. His parents felt it would be inappropriate to live a life of luxury when so many were suffering.

As he grew, he was free to roam where he wanted, unsupervised—his parents gave him plenty of love, tinged with enough freedom to create an independent spirit. He often explored forbidden places, where the mystery and danger made his heart beat fast. He liked that feeling. He often roamed the streets, getting into minor trouble. At times, he felt a connectedness to his birthplace, the African continent, like there was something or someone nearby that made him feel... whole. Other times, he didn't feel complete, like a piece of him was missing. A very important piece. He couldn't figure out what it was, not for a long time. There was a brief time where he didn't feel the longing for this piece of himself. His emptiness wasn't as empty as usual. Strange.

When his loneliness was unbearable, he felt more out of place. It was more than just where he lived, it was how he experienced life and his whole existence. He could have lived anywhere and the loneliness would still exist. This was his experience and for him it was normal.

It was a cooler than normal night, a relief from the searing heat of the day. The wind picked up, scattering leaves and garbage through the streets. A storm was moving in.

It was bedtime and he came bounding at full speed into the bedroom. He was wearing an old pair of blue footie pajamas, almost too small for him. He immediately jumped up on the bed, leaping higher and higher, trying to touch the ceiling. *They have the best bed!* A guest was staying in his room for the night, and he had been sent to sleep in his parents' room. Not an unusual occurrence—in fact, very common in their household. Other people involved with the church often stayed at the house. He fell down on the bed, laughing. He was happy to have the room to himself.

The white lace curtains were fluttering from the breeze coming through the open window. *It's going to rain.* He could smell the rain coming. It was the rainy season and the downpours came often.

He skipped to the window and looked down to the street and saw a man. The man was dirty and unshaven and was slowly struggling to cover himself in palm leaves, preparing himself for sleep. A very different sleep from his own. He stared, wondering who the man was, because he hadn't seen him before. The man suddenly looked up at him and, to his horror, he saw the man was missing an eye. It had been gouged out, leaving only an ugly scar and presumably empty socket. He gasped and couldn't help but keep staring.

The man yelled in his native dialect, "What are you staring at from the comfort of your home?!"

Although he spoke mostly English, he understood the homeless man's dialect.

"N-nothing..." he stammered. "Why do you only have one eye? What happened to your other one?"

The man sneered and said, "War. I was fighting for freedom."

"Freedom from what?"

"From you and your people," the man spat back.

The boy pointed to his chest. "Not us. We are here to help," he said with pride.

"But then, why am I here in the street and you are safe and warm inside?" the man angrily replied.

He thought about this for a minute then rushed downstairs.

"Wait," he told the man.

His parents were sitting in the living room with their guest.

"Mom, Dad!" he yelled.

"Hold on. Don't interrupt without saying 'excuse me'," his father scolded lovingly.

"Excuse me, Mom and Dad," he said, panting in between words. "There is a man outside, he doesn't have a home, and I want to invite him in."

His parents glanced at each other, smiling.

"Do you think God wants you to help him?" his father asked.

The boy stayed silent. He was not sure what he believed in, and he was definitely unsure if he believed in God.

"I'm sure he does..." the boy mumbled under his breath. "Son, do you not have faith that God would want you to help that man?"

"I have faith that I want to help that man. God does not matter."

A flash of anger crossed his father's face, which his father tried quickly to hide. But the boy could tell. He knew how his father felt about the word of God. It was absolute. He knew his father did not understand why he questioned everything.

"Son, God takes care of everyone, but we have to set an example. If we don't have faith in him, how can he help us and others?"

"Dad, I will have faith in God. I think we need to help this man," the boy whispered.

"Go, invite him in," ordered his father, knowing very well that the boy was only trying to placate him.

The boy opened the door and ran to the man, who was cocooned in his palm leaves, using an old sack as a pillow.

The boy nudged the man. "Come inside. We have food and a bed."

The man looked up at him. "Food? Bed? Yes."

The man pushed the leaves aside, awkwardly stood up, and followed the boy into the house. His parents welcomed him and led him to the kitchen, where the cook had set out some meat and rice, along with some hard bread. The man sat down and grabbed at the food, ripping the bread apart and tearing at the meat with his hand and fork simultaneously. He finished quickly. The boy's parents had left the kitchen, so the boy was there alone, staring at the man in amazement at how speedily the food disappeared.

"I was hungry," stated the man. "Do you have anything to drink? I'm thirsty."

"Do you want some water?"

"How about beer?" The man winked and smiled.

Although his parents didn't drink, they always kept some beer for their many guests.

"OK," said the boy as he opened the fridge and reached hesitantly inside. He wasn't sure if he should give the man a beer, but he didn't want to be rude.

He handed the man the bottle. The man grabbed the bottle and chugged it quickly, then he opened his mouth and let out a huge burp. The boy laughed.

"Another?" asked the man.

"OK." The boy reached for another beer.

In the course of twenty minutes, the man drank four beers and was clearly drunk. He fell out of his chair, then stood up, swaying from side to side. He walked over to the corner and started urinating. The boy was frightened.

"No, no, stop!" the boy screamed.

His parents, hearing the clattering commotion from the other room, came running into the kitchen. They were shocked to see the man urinating, visibly drunk, and on the verge of falling over.

"Stop!" screamed his father, as he grabbed the man by the coat sleeve.

Even though his father was normally patient and kind, this was clearly too much for him. He pushed the homeless man toward the door.

"It's time for you to leave."

"Fuck you!" bellowed the man. "I'm staying here tonight."

Again, the father pushed the man toward the door, this time more forcefully.

"Ahhhhh!!" The man threw a hard punch to his father's jaw, knocking him back onto the kitchen table, which came crashing down from his weight. His father was stunned.

"Stop! Please, stop!" his mother screamed at the man, who opened the fridge, searching for another beer. She quickly moved to tend to her husband. The boy sat on the floor crying. Other people came through door, the guest and some neighbors, and finally, with difficulty, they were able to roll the man outside.

The man stood up and walked down the street, cursing back at them, calling them "white colonialists." He then grabbed his palm leaves and walked down the street, away from the small yellow house.

Inside, his father was bleeding from a deep cut to his face. They determined he needed to go to the hospital.

"Stay here. It will be OK." His mother gently stroked his cheek and said, "It's OK."

She helped his father get in the car, and they left for the hospital.

The boy was stunned. He wanted to help the man. His father said God wanted him to help the man. He helped the man and now his house was a mess and his father was on his way to the hospital.

The boy, still in his blue pajamas, ran outside, looking for the man. He saw him stumbling across the street, with his pants half down.

"Hey!" yelled the boy. "Hey! You hurt my father. We and God wanted to help you!"

The man turned around with a look of hatred and rage on his face and sneered, "God? *God?* There is no God. If there were a God, would I be here on the street in the first place? Would so many people in this country, in this world, be suffering like we are? Would God have let me punch your father?"

THE MEETING

I *really don't want to go on this date.* I hated to cancel at the last minute though—that would be rude—but I had been secretly hoping that he would text and say he couldn't make it. No dice. I am on my way to the bar and already thinking this will be just another waste of time. Another boring or annoying date, no chemistry, no connection. At least occasionally I did meet some interesting men. That almost made up for all the bad dates. Why was online dating so difficult? You chatted before you met and if you found something in common, you would get together, hoping for that elusive chemistry. To me, that is paramount. And I can tell within five minutes of meeting someone if there will even be a second date. So here I am, going to meet a man and already thinking it will end in disappointment, forcing me to sneak out early with some lame excuse about my sick son.

When we chatted online, we discovered we had a lot in common. He seemed interesting, not your average man. Average was overrated. He had an unconventional life, like mine. Born in Africa, the child of missionaries, he had a very unique and interesting childhood, again just like mine. Since I also had lived in Africa for two years, I felt a strong connection to the experiences I had there. Africa holds a special place in my heart. That was probably the main reason I was interested in meeting him. My experiences in Africa gave me a different perspective on life and the world. My unusual parents, who were not missionaries but agnostic, saving-the-world hippies, made for quite an adventurous and sometimes annoying childhood. I was curious to hear about his life, his time in Africa. I thought we could share views and trade stories. I do not expect any kind of connection. My frustration level with online dating is at its max.

There he is. I see him sitting at a table, near the bar. I see him before he sees me. *He looks nervous.* He looks up and waves, and I wave back. I scan him quickly as I walk over. He isn't really what I expected (online dates never are) but then I realize I actually didn't know what to expect. He is not the type of guy I usually click "yes" to; his pictures were a bit blurry and I swiped right on a weird whim. He is attractive though; short dark hair, beautiful blue eyes. I sense a depth in his eyes—mystery or aloofness? Or maybe he is just the serious type. Or introverted. I'm not sure I see anything in his body language. *Strange.*

After we introduce ourselves, I sit down and tell him right off the bat.

"Sorry, but I can only stay for a little bit. My son is pretty sick, and I should probably get home to make sure he's OK," I lie, feeling immediately guilty when he flashes a beautifully honest smile. He seems like a genuinely nice guy.

"No problem," he replies.

We talk a lot, about many things—our childhoods, current lives, kids. We still have many things in common, but I don't feel any chemistry whatsoever. It seems unlikely that I will go out with him again. *Sigh. More wasted time. Should I go out on a second date? What if I'm wrong?* The thoughts are already spinning through my head, and he is talking. *What did he just say?* I feel slightly confused for some reason. *Nope, no second date,* I decide. *How long before I can leave?* I sit here thinking I need to speak up soon about my son being sick so I can leave. Although he is interesting and seems kind... Again my thoughts swing back and forth.

"So what do you do?" I ask.

"I work for the government," he replies. "Tech stuff. I was in the military for many years, then moved into a desk job."

"Military?" I ask, maybe with too much of a hint of judgment.

"Yes, but I'm a liberal," he replies quickly and adamantly.

I guess he gets that a lot.

Phew. Someone with opposite political views would be difficult for me. I always thought there were probably very few liberal career military, but I can't judge since I don't have any direct experience. My liberal upbringing, combined with my own very strong feelings about the barbarity of war in general, shaped my view of the military as a "war machine." In reality, those on the front lines have little say. They are simply following orders and are not in a position to determine if an action is "right" or "wrong." I am not judging him for his military service, but rather for his political views. I'd always associated staunch support of the military with political conservativism. I need to be more open-minded.

"Really?" I ask, surprised.

"What do you expect? I'm the son of missionaries!" he laughs.

I smile. *Sense of humor, that's good.*

Another stereotype shattered. My agnostic parents would condemn the missionaries and their work as forcing their ideals on people, but again I keep an open mind.

I have one drink and announce I need to leave. Sick son. I feel guilty.

He asks for my phone number, also asking if we could go out again. I stop for one second, wanting to say no, but then change my mind and say yes. *I will have to tell him at some point that I don't want to go out with him again. I can do that later.* We exchange phone numbers and say goodbye.

As I leave the bar, I decide that he is nice enough, but without that chemistry, it is pointless. I really did enjoy spending time with him. Part of me was hoping he wouldn't contact me again, not only because I hate having to tell guys that I don't want to see them again (I'm chicken shit about conflict), but also, I felt I *should* go out with him again. Very strange. I didn't know exactly what prompted my certainty, but the moment I got into my car, I knew I would go out with him again. Ah, if I could have read the future back then, I might have avoided that second date...

II

SACRED BOND

MARY MAGDALENE & JESUS

Many sins are forgiven her because she has loved very much.
~ Philip Pullman, The Good Man Jesus and the Scoundrel Christ

"Mary Magdalene Speaks:
We walked together
our souls united in the quest
for truth
He a man of flesh
yet in his beautiful eyes
eternity's love shone out
to our world
I loved him
He belongs now to the ages
You and I shall never forget
his beautiful light"
~ Ramon Ravenswood, Icons Speak

I think they probably got it on, Jesus and Mary Magdalene.
~ Madonna

Jesus travelled through towns and villages, preaching and spreading his enlightened teachings of love and unity. His messages conveyed the importance of connecting with our inner self, other humans, and the universe. He professed empathy for others and the philosophy that each person has a unique purpose to make a difference in the world. Most of his message was misinterpreted, and eventually over time, the true message he shared was obscured, becoming clouded by stories and myths.

Sensing a presence at the top of hill, Mary glanced up and was instantly blinded. A figure enfolded in a brilliant, luminous light was moving toward her. She took a deep breath and released a deep sigh, which was carried across the sand toward Jesus. She turned around and continued on her way; she was already late.

Jesus sensed the ethereal droplets of light, like a misty shower of energy, as they gently fell on his skin. He sped up to catch up to her. Mary, hearing the footsteps, turned back and saw him. Jesus softly touched her shoulder in greeting. In that instant, there was a knowing. Inexplicable. Mary was overwhelmed by the intensity of the feeling and immediately pulled away. Jesus smiled.

Before he had a chance to speak, several loud and enraged men charged toward Jesus and Mary.

"Get away from him!" one of them yelled at Mary, as he roughly pushed her aside.

Mary's face turned red and she was furious. She wanted to stand up to the men, tell them to stop treating her like a dog. She controlled herself but gave the men an indignant look as she moved away from the group. She watched Jesus out of the corner of her eye, wary.

Jesus smiled at her. "We will meet again."

Mary felt confused as the men moved away. *Who is this man?* She walked the rest of the way home wondering about the feeling she had when he touched her. There was a familiarity. Had she met him before? Her mind raced, trying to remember when she might have met him. By the time she arrived home, it was dark. She looked up and saw a bright light shoot across the sky. She had seen one before. She didn't know what it was, but it was beautiful.

She couldn't stop thinking about the man. She knew him from somewhere. She knew him as well as she knew herself, even though she knew nothing about him. Was she losing her mind? Shimmery objects in the sky and now this? She felt interwoven in the fabric of his being and his memories. *No, we are knit together.* She remembered the way his hand felt when he touched her, the warmth, and felt a deep need to find that warmth again. Mary slept soundly that night, dreaming of a brilliant light, enveloped by its comforting rays.

I'm late. Mary rushed to the market, so she could get back home and prepare the evening meal. She turned the corner to the village square. She stopped. The man was standing by the water well, addressing a small crowd. She closed her eyes and listened. She was mesmerized by his poetic verses.

Even though Jesus' back was turned to her, he sensed her presence immediately. He turned around. She opened her eyes, knowing he was looking at her. When she saw the soft expression on his face, the tenderness in his eyes, she recognized that he loved her. It was beyond words, beyond normal understanding. Just a knowing. And in that moment, she realized that she loved him in return.

Someone called out, "Jesus, keep talking."

Jesus. She recognized his name. The stories about him had circulated for months in the village. *He is important and on* a mission. *And this mission has nothing to do with me.* She knew she needed to keep her distance.

"Mary." He approached her. "I know you. "

"And I know you," she replied quietly.

As they gazed at one another, inhaling as if to remember the moment, they both saw sparks of light emanating from their chests, from their hearts. The sparks turned into a solid, pure white, luminous light. It was familiar to both, although Mary did not have a specific recollection of the light; only that she had experienced it before. She held her hand out, and Jesus took it, grasping her hand gently in both of his. They felt a sense of familiarity and love. Nostalgia? Even Jesus, who knew exactly what was happening, was shocked at the magnitude of the emotions. He knew he must not be pulled too far into her energy. He had a purpose beyond earthly pleasures. Mary felt these same emotions of familiarity and a strong magnetic attraction towards him; she desired to be closer to him and couldn't break away. *We cannot be more than what we are,* she thought.

He replied aloud, "Yes, yes. I have something I must do before I leave the world, something of importance that will influence all of mankind."

An incredible collective sadness engulfed them. They both sensed each other's pain; both felt the immense feeling of despair. In their connectedness, they could feel each other, like they were one soul.

She told him, *I will be here for you. I will help you with your mission.*

Yes, he replied, *I would like that. And I need you.*

All of this was said without either one speaking aloud.

Mary turned and walked away, finishing her errands and hurrying home. The pain felt impossible to erase.

Mary was consumed with longing for him, desiring the connection, physically, emotionally, and spiritually. She slowly began to unravel. Her emotions overpowered her logic, making everything feel out of balance. She felt like she was tumbling into a dark abyss, entangled, losing her sense of clarity. The darkness firmly set in; she fell into a deep depression. *Help. Help me.*

He found her huddled against the wall, knees drawn in, staring at nothing. Her face was stained with old tears.

"Mary," he whispered, "I was wakened from a dream. A black fog was surrounding you. Listen to me." He gently lifted her chin and looked into her eyes. "Do not feel sorry for yourself, for me, for us. You have to be strong. Find that strength. Push back the darkness. Fight."

We cannot be together in this lifetime. That is for the future, in another life. We will be together in another life.

The words offered her little comfort. She tried to understand and absorb what he was saying. Her mind understood, but her heart refused to comprehend.

She stared at him blankly, no emotion in her eyes.

Jesus placed his hands on her shoulders, sending the light directly to the centers overwhelmed with negative emotions.

Her eyelids fluttered briefly, then her eyes slowly closed. She slept a deep, dreamless, healing sleep.

She awakened refreshed, the night before just a foggy memory. All she remembered was a dream, Jesus touched her, *here*, and she felt something pass through her. She smiled. She remembered she had work to do with Jesus today and dressed quickly.

Days passed, they traveled to many towns—Jesus, his followers, and Mary, the only woman among them. She knew how the others felt, but she didn't care anymore. This was what she was meant to do.

A day Mary knew in her heart would come finally arrived. *It was only a matter of time. They hate him.*

The Romans saw Jesus as an insurgent that needed to be eliminated. It happened quickly. She watched in horror and sorrow as Jesus was beaten and crucified, nailed to a wooden cross by his hands and feet.

She looked up at him. *Are you suffering?*

His face was solemn, stoic, a betrayal of his actual pain. She saw there was pain, she felt it in her own body: *My heart is fractured.* However, she did not weep. *He is strong, otherworldly.* Kneeling now, she watched in silence as his body surrendered, as his soul left the physical plane. She laid her head in the dirt and sobbed. Her light love, her soul connection, her spirit lover, was gone. She would have to live the rest of her days without his presence.

His disciples released Jesus' body from the crucifix and secretly buried their leader in a cave. The tomb was sealed with an enormous stone to prevent the Romans from discovering the body.

A few days passed. Mary had avoided the cave, fearing the emotions that would arise. But now she was ready. She knew his light was no longer present, only his body, an empty vessel. But she believed she could speak to him and that he would hear her, so she made her way to his tomb.

What? The heavy stone door had been moved. *Impossible!*

She peered inside the cave. It was dark and musty, but she could tell right away that it was empty. Jesus' body was gone. Her first thought was that the Romans had discovered it. *Where is his body?!*

She felt a chill run up her back and the hairs on her arms stand up. She sensed something—a presence? Hesitantly, she turned around.

"Jesus," she gasped, falling to her knees, stunned.

He was surrounded by a white glow, brighter than any light she had witnessed emanating from him while he lived. The light encompassed him.

She rose and moved toward him, reached out her hand. Jesus stopped her.

I am ascending to the light soon, he told her.

Please, take me with you! she pleaded.

Jesus smiled. *No, it is not yet your time. We will know each other in many other lives. We will not remember who we were, but we will have a sense of knowing and connection. In spirit, we will always be connected, even if our physical bodies are not. One day we will be ready in both body and soul and on that day, all that we have forgotten will be remembered.*

He smiled one last time, looked at her, and ascended into the light.

DEEP COMMUNION

If there is magic on this planet, it is contained in water.
~ Loren Eiseley

The wave does not need to die to become water. She is already water.
~ Thich Nhat Hanh

The full moon rose over the park. Children laughed and skipped through the newly mowed grass, ignoring the paved pathways. Young couples sat on benches, in the darkest corners of the park, secretly holding hands and sometimes even touching lips. Patrons sat at the café across the street, sipping "cafezinhos" or cold beers, the men glancing at their watches, wondering if it was time to find their wives, before the wives found them. Many came to the park. Women with babies, who one day would run with the other children. Grandmothers knitted, frowning with disapproval at the young couples on the benches. Palm trees dotted the park, and large, oval lamps lit the center of the square, veiling the fringes in mystery. The children played games, mostly hide and seek, discovering perfect hiding places in the dimly lit areas of the park. Loud, giggling voices rose above the calm and quite adult conversation.

"My turn to count!" shouted a small boy. "Everyone hide!"

The children scattered like frightened chickens, squawking and squealing and bumping into one another. Dresses that had once been starched and white were now dirty and crumpled as the children scurried to find the best hiding places.

She jumped down to the most coveted spot—a tiny ledge overlooking a path of steps that led down to the ocean. A boy tried to slide in next to her, but she pushed him away and he left, knowing that the first to reach the spot was the supreme ruler. She squatted down on the ledge, a few steps above the water. It was low tide and bright enough for her to see the hole in the wall that supposedly ran under the city.

It was rumored that many years ago, pirates dug a tunnel under the old city, burying a huge treasure and then escaping back out to sea. They planned to one day claim their booty, but they never returned and supposedly somewhere under the city, beneath the catacombs, was an enormous treasure. All those who searched for the treasure died when the tide mysteriously came in, sweeping the treasure hunters to their watery deaths. *I will be brave enough one day to go in that hole and I will find the treasure. Then I'll be rich and can do whatever and go wherever I want.*

She shivered slightly as a cool breeze whisked up the surf. The waves calmly and gently washed up over the rocks below. She sat staring at the water, daydreaming about her future, when she suddenly heard her name. Thinking she had been found, she glanced up toward the top of the sea wall. *Nobody there.* She heard her name yet again and realized the voice was not coming through her ears. It was in her head, as well as in her heart; she sensed the vibration on her skin. The water—she knew this intuitively. *The water is calling to me.*

She cautiously walked down the two remaining steps; the stairs were slippery. Gently, yet with some hesitation, she slipped her fingertips into the cool water. Electric and wild. She fearfully pulled her hand out.

Why does the water feel so funny? So...hot? It burns. But, yet, it doesn't burn. Although she was frightened, she cautiously immersed her hand back in the water. Again, she felt the same currents of heat over her hand. The heat soon began to change to euphoria, pure freedom. She couldn't quite make sense of the feeling or put it into words, but she seemed to understand intuitively what it meant. She was completely open, giving herself to the sea. She sensed the sea studying her, learning who she was. Release, the sea could release her, free her from all that sadness that permeated her life on Earth and she would be free to swim in the sea, wrapped in the soothing lining of the surf. She was welcome. The sea seduced her and drew her into his arms.

"NO!" she screamed and immediately pulled her hand out of the water. "No, I don't want to go. I want to stay here. Here, on land, where I was born. I can't survive in the sea. I'll die!"

She expectantly looked down at the ocean, waiting for some response, but none came. The ocean was silent. She took a deep breath and tentatively dipped her small pinky finger into the water, just barely breaking the surface. *Nothing.* She decidedly pushed the rest of her hand in, and this time felt the warmth.

The sea spoke to her.

There is nothing to be afraid of, for I do not take those who do not want to be part of me. It is in your blood to love me.

What you feel are memories. There is an interwoven tapestry of infinite memories, shared through the water. You are remembering the past and living the future. I am a part of something larger. We are all connected.

Then silence. She kept her hand in the water for a few more minutes, but the voice had disappeared.

Later that night, she lay in her bed listening to the waves, the peaceful ebb and flow, a whispering, reassuring lullaby. A soothing sea. She wondered about her encounter earlier, whether it was her imagination, whether she was going crazy. *I imagine too much.* She was always looking toward the future, envisioning her departure from the island. Picturing herself many years from now, on her own, free. *I will find what I'm seeking; I will find what has been lost.* She fell asleep, lulled by the waves, drawn gently into a dream, a dream of water, and a boy.

FEAR
OF DROWNING

Love is like water. We can fall in it.
We can drown in it. And we can't live without it.
~ Unknown

He walked along the beach, the waves breaking over the sand and a salty smell permeating the air. In the distance, the boy noticed a cargo ship as it glided toward an unknown destination, carrying goods to a foreign country. He imagined that it was going around the Cape of Good Hope, through stormy seas. The boy watched as the ship slowly made its way across the horizon. *I wish I could be on that ship.*

Suddenly he remembered. *The shipwreck.* Many years ago, a massive cargo ship ran aground on some rocks and washed up on the shore. The metal carcass was never moved. He ran toward it, impulsive and excited. He was not allowed to go there—it was dangerous, said his parents. He went anyway. The excitement, the danger, beckoned him. He wanted to explore, look for treasure and dark secrets. The other boys ran to catch up with him, barefoot, just as he was, although he went barefoot by choice.

The boys cautiously entered through a lower window and carefully climbed onto the rusty, creaking ship. It was dark inside, and he heard the waves slapping at the sides of the large metal carcass, a rhythmic drumming, a reminder of the ocean's presence. He ran ahead of the other boys, jumping over debris, sprinting upstairs, and through several doorways. He had explored the ship many times and had memorized the route. Suddenly he found himself alone. He stopped. It was nearly pitch-black, with small slivers of sunlight sneaking through the cracks in the frame of the ship. He was panting.

He cupped his hands over his mouth and shouted, "Hello!"

He listened, waiting for the echo.

Hello... Hello... Hello... the ship echoed back.

He stepped into a cabin and found an old, cracked mirror. He stared at his reflection, a small, skinny boy, dirty, stubborn, *that's what my father says.* There was a sudden fleeting flicker in the corner of the mirror. A shadow? He felt the air move as something quickly passed behind him. He screamed and whipped around. Nothing there. He must have imagined it.

A bit shaken, he exited the cabin and returned to the cavernous engine room, the echo chamber, as he called it. He heard the waves as they rhythmically drummed the metal ship. It felt soothing and he closed his eyes. Thump, thump, thump. The thumping stopped and he heard a voice. Without hesitation, he knew it was the waves. He wasn't quite sure how that crazy thought even popped into his head. *Waves can't speak.*

He heard a voice again, this time very clearly.

I am a connection to everything since the beginning of time. You will return home. Her light lives on in these waters.

The words filled his head.

He turned in a full circle around the room, searching for the source of the voice.

Her? What are you talking about?

Come, come to the window, the voice beckoned.

He slowly stepped toward the open window, cautiously because the water was much higher on that side of the ship. Looking out the window, he saw the cargo ship as it continued making its way across the horizon.

Reach down and touch the water, the ocean coaxed.

He swallowed. His hands were shaking; he was uncertain. He felt a tinge of fear, but the fear was also tinged with excitement. He reached out the window and down to the cold water below.

Instantly, he felt it. An electric heat, a connection, something intermixed in the salt and seaweed filled with energy, light, and knowledge.

He was stunned by the sensation. All at once he was filled with both love and terror.

I'm out of here.

He ran through the maze of doorways, stairs, and hallways, somehow remembering his way back to the beach. He exited through the large gaping hole and collided with his friends. He fell down on the sand, his eyes wide and full of fear, and started to tell them what happened.

"I..." he stopped. *They'll think I'm crazy.*

He sat there in the sand, panting, unable to speak.

"What's the matter? Can't talk? Scared of the dark?" the boys teased.

"Shut up!" He pushed one of the boys and ran off down the beach. He kept running, until he was far away from the boys, far from the ship, separated from the mysterious voice.

It was a dream. That's all it was. A daydream.

He shook himself to clear his head and headed home.

FIRST CONTACT

t's early Monday morning. I can't sleep, as usual, so I decide
to get up and make some coffee. I'm tired. I went to bed too
late last night. The early bird in me should know better. At least
my son is with his dad this week, so I don't have to deal with
waking a cranky teenager.

I look over at my phone and see a text from my date from last
night.

Him: Good morning!

That's thoughtful. And sweet.

Him: I'd like to see you again when you're free.

I don't reply right away. I'm still not sure I want to go out
with him again. Yes or no? I intuitively decide yes.

Me: Good morning! That would be great. I'm free any day
this week.

Him: OK, how about Wednesday, dinner?

We agree to dinner on Wednesday at six. I'm still hesitant,
but I feel like I should see him. Should... I'm not a "should" sort
of person anymore. I go with it though.

He texts me again later that day to say hello. And several
times over the next couple of days. *How thoughtful is that?* Still,
I am slightly uneasy by all the communication and attention. Too

much. He makes me laugh. I should really like him. I'm just not used to all the attention. Not in a long time anyway. He seems thoughtful and is willing to show that he's interested. What is holding me back? He texts me again in the evening.

Him: Sweet dreams!

And I momentarily melt.

The next day brings a change. He needs to move dinner to Thursday so he can see his kids on Wednesday. OK, I'm good with that. More time to deliberate. However, Thursday comes and yet another change. Dinner is now a drink and a bit later because of another conflict. Oh boy. I'm annoyed at this point and I'm hoping that he cancels entirely.

Changes in plans are not a huge thing, but I'm starting to feel that things are too complicated already and that's not a good sign. I realize things come up, but this seems to irritate me quite a bit. Why am I sensing complications and issues with just this one little thing? I'm a little confused by my feelings, but I feel pulled to go out with him anyway and tell myself to not worry about the future. I am guessing he may even make another change before tonight.

Thursday afternoon, details in place, I wait for the cancellation. Am I hoping for it or fearing it? Both. He does not cancel.

The sound of live music greets me as I arrive at the restaurant, a quaint, although overpriced, little inn. I'm happy. This is one of my favorite places, and the music, coupled with the unusually warm fall weather, makes for a perfect evening. We say our hellos and grab an outside table near the bar.

It's an easy conversation and we talk more about ourselves, our lives, and delve into a more personal discussion about past pains and future dreams. I'm feeling very comfortable, as if I have known him for far longer than two days. I talk freely and don't even think about what I'm going to say next, which I am apt to do a lot. I'm telling him about my acting experiences in New York, my #MeToo encounter with an infamous director. As I'm getting toward the end of my story, he leans over, puts his hand on top of mine, and kisses me.

There is something in that simple kiss, that slight touch, that completely stuns me. I feel an electrical current run through me, like a romantic heroine in a classical novel. I am overwhelmed. Overpowered. I know who he is. It's him. This is insane... *He is the one*, is all I can think. He is the man who has been haunting my dreams my entire life. I feel like I have been waiting for this moment, the kiss, as if I knew it was going to happen. I cannot explain why. We continue to kiss, softly. I feel like I am being pulled into him, into something undefined, like a magnet. There is a definitive connection beyond anything I have ever experienced. I know, in this very moment, that I love him. I feel whole. I am at peace. I am home.

He asks me if I want another drink and I say yes. While he is at the bar, all I can think about is the power of that kiss. I can't believe this is happening to me. He comes back, sits down, and immediately kisses me again and whispers, "I'm not afraid."

I stop. *What? What the hell does that mean?* I look at him but I don't say anything. I briefly wonder if this is a red flag.

Completely. Anyone that kisses you and at the same time says they are not afraid, obviously means they *are* afraid. *He* is afraid. What is he afraid of? What does he mean? Why don't I ask? It's too late at this point. I was already all in at the first kiss. So I ignore it.

He suggests we continue the night, as the bar begins to close. I impulsively invite him to my place, since I live nearby. I clearly tell him that there is nothing implied in the invitation, that I'm not going to sleep with him, that we can just have another drink and talk. In all honesty, I desperately want to sleep with him. What will the connectedness feel like when our bodies touch? No, it's too soon. I have an endless argument going on in my head as I get in my car. Yes, no, yes, no, sex, no sex, yes, yes, yes, sex, sex, sex... My moral, practical self loses.

He follows in his car and two very strange things happen. First, he gets pulled over for having a headlight out, which I hadn't even noticed. He gets a ticket. Then, as soon as we get back on the road, he gets a flat tire. I wish I believed in signs—these seem like sure signs of *turn around and do not take him home with you*. I laugh at the thought. They are just coincidences.

One thing leads to another and he stays the night. I wake in the middle of the night, thinking about how blissful I feel. The connection was amplified, like nothing I had ever experienced. The immensity and intenseness of the experience was beyond explanation and I couldn't find the words even in my imagination to describe the way I felt. It was like past, present, and future emotions all blended together. I still can't believe I met him. I fall fast asleep, my leg draped over his body.

After he leaves the next morning, I decide I am all in. No fear—I am vulnerable and open. I cannot contain myself. This is what I have waited for my entire life. I feel complete; I am home. I listen to all my favorite songs in the car, sing, sing at the top of my lungs, all the emotions coming out in my voice. This is one of my favorite things to do when I'm happy. I feel like I'm singing loudly and passionately enough that the whole world can hear me. Love, happiness, an amazing thing to have happened to me. Just when I thought it was impossible.

BROKEN

TRISTAN
AND ISOLDE

*...for most men are unaware that what is in the
power of magicians to accomplish,
that the heart can also accomplish by dint of love and bravery.*
~ M. Joseph Bédier, The Romance of Tristan and Iseult

Isolde: How many have you loved before me?
Tristan: None.
Isolde: And after me?
Tristan: None.
~ Tristan and Isolde (Movie, 2006)

Tristan swung left, then lifted the sword over his head and brought it down on Morholt. He was exhausted, and this was finally done. Morholt's demand of tribute was not happily received by King Mark of Cornwall, and Tristan had been sent to fight Morholt in single combat. As Tristan bent to clean his sword, he winced and noticed he was also injured, a slice in his leg. *Ah, it will heal. Just need to get back home.*

Despite his positive affirmations, the wound refused to heal. He suffered in agony until he heard of someone who could heal any wound. The only problem was the healer also happened to be Queen Isolde, Morholt's sister. Not wanting to be recognized, Tristan traveled in disguise to the home of King Anguish and Queen Isolde in Ireland. His condition continued to worsen and he was near death when they finally anchored in a small cove near the castle.

He told his crew to place him alone inside a small boat, with food, water, and his harp, and push the boat to shore. He then ordered them to leave the cove. As he lay in pain on the bottom of the boat, moving gradually closer to shore, he slowly played his harp. The melodious music carried to the shore and the local people were drawn to the drifting boat.

"Who are you?" asked a villager.

Tristan lied, "I am a court minstrel. I was kidnapped and injured by pirates and left at sea to die."

"You shall not die today! We will take you to the queen," proclaimed the villager. And with that, the villagers picked up Tristan and carried him to Queen Isolde's castle.

Queen Isolde insisted on questioning him before she would heal him.

"Minstrel, I hear you play the harp beautifully. Will you play for me?" asked the queen.

Tristan played a short measure, but he grew tired quickly and stopped.

"You are gravely injured. What is your name?" Queen Isolde demanded.

Tristan thought quickly. "My name is Tantris."

Queen Isolde looked at him and saw an opportunity.

"Tantris, I can heal you, but only if you promise to teach your musical skills to my daughter."

"Yes," whispered Tristan, barely able to speak.

When Tristan was well enough, he started tutoring Princess Isolde, who was named after her mother.

Isolde was beautiful. Tristan sensed something magical, a compelling, immense magnetism in her presence. The instant he saw her, he was overcome with love. Intermingled with the love was a sense of sadness though, because of his deception and the knowledge that he would need to leave one day. *I must hide these feelings.*

"Princess Isolde, pay attention. What are you daydreaming about?" He was frustrated—she had been in another place all morning. Usually she played the harp beautifully.

Isolde was most definitely in another place, somewhere she did not want him to know about. Ever since she met Tantris, she felt drawn to him. Not just his looks, but his spark, his light, if there was such a thing. Isolde felt like she had known him all her life. She wanted him, wanted him in a way that confused her. She imagined herself running her hands over his muscular body, feeling the heat of his skin... She stopped herself. She had to focus. But she was curious about him. He was hiding something; she knew it.

"Tantris, where are you from again? And how did you know to come to my mother to heal you?" she asked coyly.

"I told you, I am from a land across the sea, a cold, icy place where there are big, white bears and the sun doesn't shine for six months." He did not look at her, for fear that she would sense his lies.

She smiled and batted her eyes. "What is the name of the place?"

"Smorkjen. It's small; you will not have heard of it. There are very few people from my country who have ventured beyond the borders." He hoped that was enough. It usually was.

"Well, how did you find my mother?" she asked.

"I was coming ashore to die; I didn't want to die at sea and ran into some villagers who brought me to her. I surely would have perished if not for their charity."

"Don't you want to go home?"

Tristan paused. No, he did not want to go home. He wanted to stay with Isolde, take her in his arms, love her, and stay with her until his death.

He looked away from her and whispered, "No, I am happy here. For now."

Time passed and Tristan's wounds had nearly healed. He knew he could not stay any longer, so close to Isolde, without being able to ever truly express his love for her. He approached Queen Isolde and told her he needed to leave; he had a beloved wife at home, and it was time to return. He knew this lie was the only way Queen Isolde would allow him to go.

"Tantris, I am saddened, but the vows of marriage are sacred, and you must return to your wife," she answered.

"Thank you, Queen Isolde, I will be forever grateful for your kind gesture." He bowed, quickly packed his few possessions, and left immediately, not even saying goodbye to Princess Isolde. It pained him to do this, but he knew it was the only way he could escape without weakening and confessing his love for her.

Tristan was welcomed back a hero by King Mark for his triumph over Morholt. The only ones not pleased were the barons. They were angry at his return. They mistrusted Tristan and feared he was conspiring in some way to place himself on King Mark's throne. The barons constantly attempted to discredit Tristan, whispering lies in the King's ear, accusing Tristan of deceit and treachery. King Mark refused to believe the barons' words and ordered them to stop questioning Tristan's loyalty immediately.

"It will not end well for you if you continue with such treachery!" threatened the king.

"Tristan! You return a hero. Tell me, are the stories true? How did you manage to win the trust of the king and queen, after defeating her brother Morholt?" asked King Mark.

"Your Majesty, I posed as a minstrel, seeking healing. The Queen Isolde so loved my music, she offered to heal me, but only if I stayed on to tutor her daughter in music." Isolde. Her memory stopped him for a moment. *I miss her.*

He continued. "Thus, I stayed on, becoming a trusted teacher."

"Tell me about the Princess Isolde," said King Mark.

Tristan paused, reflecting on Isolde's beauty.

"There are no words to describe her beauty. Her hair, golden like the sun, flows down upon a face more lovely and fair than any I have ever seen. She is also a gifted musician, naturally playing the harp as if it were part of her. The notes...they speak directly from her soul."

He ceased talking.

The memory of her was too much. He had to stop contemplating her because a union with her was impossible.

"Oh?" King Mark was instantly intrigued, sensing the emotion behind Tristan's description. "Is she betrothed to anyone?"

Tristan felt uneasy with King Mark's questions regarding Isolde, but he continued.

"I am not sure, Your Majesty. I'm sure if not, she will be soon. There are few that would escape being single with such beauty, not to mention royal ties."

King Mark pondered this. He needed to form a tie with this court and, although he had decided he would not marry, his mind was wandering at the possibility of taking the unique woman as his bride. The marriage would create a powerful alliance. The kingdoms were mortal enemies, and the bond of marriage would create a truce. But how would he convince the King and Queen of Ireland that their daughter should marry him?

"Tristan, I want to wed this woman. I'm sending you to Ireland to praise my virtues and convince the king and queen to let me wed their daughter and thus create an alliance between our two kingdoms. No longer will we be enemies." He spoke excitedly and ordered Tristan to leave at once.

Tristan was shocked. He instantly regretted telling King Mark about Isolde. He wanted to scream, *No! I love her!* But he remained silent. He could not disobey his king.

Instead, Tristan politely replied to the king, "Yes, my liege. I will do as you command and promise to praise your virtues to the king and queen."

His plan was simple, although dangerous. Ireland had long been plagued by a fierce dragon and King Anguish promised the hand of his daughter to any man who killed the beast. He decided he would slay it in the name of King Mark, thus forcing the King of Ireland to give Isolde's hand to King Mark. Although the countries were enemies, the word of a king stood firm.

He arrived in Ireland and eventually encountered the dragon. After a fierce battle, he finally slew the beast and cut out its tongue as proof. What he did not realize, however, was that the poison in the tongue was highly toxic and merely putting the tongue in his cloak was dangerous. Tristan was overcome when the poison seeped through the fabric of his clothing. He weakened and collapsed in a heap by the side of the road.

King Anguish's Chief Steward came upon the dragon's corpse and, thinking of his own lecherous desires and remembering the king's proclamation regarding the dragon, he quickly gathered some witnesses and claimed that he had killed the dragon. He chopped off the dragon's head and set off to the palace, delighted that soon he would be married to the Princess Isolde.

Tristan was unable to move and was slowly falling into delirium. *I am lost. I will die here in the ditch. I will never see Isolde again.* He fell into a deep sleep, where he dreamt of two strange light beings, one male and one female. He felt the warmth of their light and sensed a great love between them. He thought he recognized them, but he couldn't see their faces clearly. He only knew that, somehow, he had met them before.

"I do not think you are telling the truth, steward," rebuked Queen Isolde. "Tell me, why did you remove the dragon's tongue? And where is it?"

"Your grace, I cut it off in battle...I...I...don't know where it is..." he stuttered nervously.

The queen looked annoyed and was about to reply, when a knight rushed in.

"Your grace! We found a man by the side of the road. He's been poisoned by dragon blood. He needs help!"

The queen's skills healed Tristan for a second time. He was overcome with guilt for his past lies and he confessed the truth. Not all of it was well received. Yes, he killed the dragon. However, he also confessed to killing Morholt. The king and queen were stunned and angry but contained their desire for revenge after Tristan's convincing promises of restitution. The king and queen eventually consented to Princess Isolde's marriage to King Mark. They understood the political benefits of the union.

Tristan had avoided contact with Isolde, boarding the ship before she did and staying out of sight. He could think of nothing else except her, but he knew he must keep those thoughts in check.

Isolde was miserable. She didn't want to marry King Mark. She was in love with Tristan. One evening, tired of sitting alone, she slipped out of her cabin to find him. She knocked softly on his door.

When Tristan opened the door, he was at once both shocked and thankful. He pulled Isolde inside, shutting the door quickly behind him.

He looked at her in silence. *Why is she tempting me, why is she tempting me?* No, no, no... He continued repeating these thoughts.

In silence, Isolde raised her hand and touched his cheek, and in that single touch, he realized he loved her more deeply than he thought possible. He lost all control. He reached out, ran his fingers through her hair, took hold of her by the waist and pulled her body against his. The burning heat, the desire, this is what he had been longing for.

"I love you, Isolde," he whispered, soft, like a sigh, his breath caressing her face.

"And I love you, Tristan."

They kissed passionately and he guided her toward the bed.

They made love and spent the next few days together in Tristan's cabin. It was risky, but their passion overcame all logic. All they could think about was the deep connection as their bodies moved together. They both understood her future husband and king was waiting for her across the sea, and they wanted to savor every moment.

"How will we see each other once I am married to the king? I don't want to marry him," she told Tristan, the night before their arrival.

"You must. I swear I will continue to love you and we will find a way to see each other. You must swear the same. You must marry the king." He stopped. "I am lost without you."

"I swear by the gods that I will always love you and will never leave your side," she declared, holding her hand over her heart. She looked at him, slid her fingers over the scars on his chest, and finally said, "Let's run away, go to Smorkjen, where nobody knows us, start a new life together!"

Tristan pushed her hand away.

"I can't, Isolde. I have a duty to my king, and you are his bride. My loyalty to him is absolute."

"Tristan! Please. I don't want to marry him, I want to marry you!" she implored, her eyes filled with tears.

He was fraught with remorse for what had to be.

"That's enough." His words were angry, though his heart was breaking.

Tristan passed her clothes to her. "Please get dressed. It's time to go." He did not dare look at her.

Isolde cried quietly. The resolute look on his face and his sudden coldness left her no choice but to dress and leave.

Once she was dressed, he opened the door and led her into the corridor.

"Guards, escort Princess Isolde to her quarters. She isn't feeling well."

She stared at him in disbelief, unable to say anything. She felt as if her heart had been cut into pieces.

"Make sure there is a guard outside her door at all times. Don't let her leave her quarters for the remainder of the trip," Tristan commanded.

I had to do it. She belonged to his king. She was not his. There was nothing more he could do. If his weakness overtook him, and he ran away with her, it would be his end. The king would find them both and kill them. And he would die a traitor.

Soon after their arrival, Isolde unhappily married King Mark. She cried throughout the entire ceremony, each time apologizing, saying she was overwhelmed with joy. The king was pleased with this response and loved her even more.

Tristan and Isolde saw each other several times over the next few weeks. They avoided looking at each other. Eventually, though, the desire was too powerful, too magnetic. One day they found themselves alone in the hallway of the tower, and passion overcame the fear of discovery; they clung to each other in desperate need.

Isolde and Tristan continued to seek one another secretly. They were careful not to get caught. The king's advisors suspected the betrayal and repeatedly tried to have the pair tried for adultery, but the couple continually evaded the accusations and preserved the farce of innocence.

Eventually, they were caught one day by the king. It was only a matter of time. The king, furious, resolved to punish them for their treachery and deceit. He immediately ordered Tristan's hanging and that Isolde be burned at the stake.

On the day of the executions, the king felt pity for Isolde and at the last moment, he changed his mind and decided instead to send Isolde to a leper colony. Tristan's execution still stood. Tristan knew what he had to do. He escaped on his way to the gallows. Although he did not want to spend a life on the run, this was the only way his survival was guaranteed. Isolde was already on her way to the leper colony, so there was no chance for a goodbye. They would never see each other again and for the rest of their lives would feel a great longing for the connection they once shared.

LOST

I am a lost soul
Wandering into my dreams
Lost and confused
A dream full of pain and screams.
~ Nishu

She grabbed the microphone and jumped on the table, singing loudly at the top of her voice to Donna Summer.

"Bad girls... talking about the sad girls!" She closed her eyes and swayed to the music.

Nobody tried to stop her; they were amused and entertained by her performance, as well as all completely drunk. She felt free, singing, sharing herself like that, in a way that was not normal to her when she was sober. Sober, she was quiet and shy and lacked confidence. But drunk, she was able to let loose the unbridled emotions that she often kept inside, hidden from others. Finally, the club owner rushed up to the table and asked her to please come down.

"*No!*" she yelled, laughing hysterically.

She pulled away from him and in the process lost her balance and began toppling backwards, still laughing. Her friend caught her before she hit the floor and the owner grabbed the microphone out of her hands.

"Hey! I'm still singing!" she said angrily. "I'm not finished, you bastard!"

She stumbled toward the club owner but before she reached him, two bouncers firmly picked her up and carried her outside.

Furious, she screamed at the owner and the staff, as well as the crowd of onlookers surrounding her who had gathered to watch the spectacle.

"I need anudda dwink," she slurred her words. "Let me in."

She attempted to go back inside the bar but was stopped by the bouncer, a man twice her size.

"No, you can't come inside. You are banned," he said in broken English, standing between her and the door.

She raised her hand toward the bouncer, but a man, a stranger, gripped her wrist and pulled her away from the crowd and the chaos.

"Come," he said, "I know a better place."

She was easily led and draped her arms around him, pushing her body close to his.

"I wanna dwink," she said.

"Anything for you, princess," he whispered in her ear and grabbed her hand, drawing it to his crotch. She didn't even flinch.

They entered a nearly empty bar. The only customer was a man who sat slumped over a table, sound asleep and snoring loudly. The dingy, dark room reeked of stale alcohol, body odor, and cigarette smoke.

"Whiskey, two," demanded the man.

She shook her head and said, "Bottle. One bottle."

He poured two very full glasses.

She reached for the bottle instead and drank, swallowing large gulps of the whiskey. Too much.

"Another..." She opened her mouth to speak, but suddenly turned and vomited. Her knees buckled and she fell to the floor, eventually lying down on the dirty, sticky floor. Then darkness.

She woke in the middle of the night naked in a strange bed, next to a strange man. Her body ached. She noticed bruises on her arms and torso. She remembered nothing. The night before could have been fun, could have been awful...she had no idea. This was not unusual for her. The man snored. *Time to leave.* She quietly climbed out of the bed and looked for her clothes, which were scattered everywhere. She dressed hurriedly and made her escape.

Where the hell am I and who is that man? I don't remember anything. Well, I'll have to ask someone what happened last night.

She walked through the dark and nearly deserted streets, unafraid of the roaming, nocturnal derelicts and strangers, walking with a comfort that demonstrated she had done this many times before. Finally, she arrived home. *Ugh. No key.* The door was locked. The window. It was the only way in. She climbed the tree, then hopped on the wall next to her house, easily reaching the window ledge, and quickly clambered up and in. She was an expert at stealthy entrances.

She took off her clothes and climbed into bed, when the lights suddenly turned on. Her parents stood in the doorway, looking concerned and upset.

"We saw you tonight, drunk, dancing on the table, singing and creating chaos," said her father. "You were out of control and we know this is not the first time. You are sixteen. You shouldn't be drinking at bars or going home with strange men. You have to stop this."

"You have a problem, with the drinking," said her mother. "We are very concerned."

She sat in silence. She didn't like this: the accusations, the intrusion into her life. She wanted a drink. There was too much pain. She needed a drink.

"You guys are always telling me what to do!" she screamed. "Leave me alone!"

She got up and shut the door, locking her parents out of her room. *And out of my life.* Crawling into her bed, she pulled the blankets over her head and cried. She felt lonely, sad, broken, unloved. All she wanted was to fit in, to feel loved and accepted. Something was missing in her life, but she couldn't define it. She drank to fill the deep void, to cover the pain, to feel whole, to feel loved. She sobbed uncontrollably.

REBEL

Every act of rebellion is a nostalgia for innocence
and an appeal to essential being.
~ Albert Camus

There was a loud crash as the glass shattered. He looked up, stunned, then turned to his friend, who was standing next to him in shock. He looked down at his hands, which were covered in blood and shaking. He couldn't remember. *Did I break the glass?* He had no memory of breaking it, but the glass from the storefront window was shattered, there were shards on the ground, and blood was dripping from his fingers. *I broke it.*

"We need to run, now!" yelled his friend.

His friend took off down the road, turned the corner, and was gone in an instant.

He stood there in shock. Looking at his bloody hands and the broken glass shards spread on the pavement, he tried to remember what had happened. He wanted to run but he couldn't move. *Why did I do this?*

"Hey, you, don't move!" a stern voice commanded from across the street.

He turned around and saw a cop. The cop hurried toward him. The boy kept staring at the cop. Then back at his hands.

"What happened here?" asked the cop.

The boy continued staring, as if in a trance.

"What happened?" the cop asked again.

As soon as the boy heard the words a second time, he came out of his daze and ran down the street, toward the park.

"Hey, kid, stop!" the cop yelled, in pursuit.

He didn't care whether the cop had pulled his gun and would shoot him; he kept running. The boy glanced back and saw that the cop was about fifty yards away. He sped up. *I have to get away. I can't get caught.* He darted wildly, leaping over boulders and zigzagging around trees. He saw a small shed ahead and it looked like the perfect hiding place. He opened the door; thankfully, it was unlocked. He stepped inside and slammed the door. He was panting and out of breath.

It was quiet.

I've lost him. I'm good.

He saw a pile of dirt and sat down, leaning against the wall of the old shed. Taking a deep, shuddering breath, he reached into his pocket for a cigarette. His hands were shaking and he could barely hold the lighter steady. Finally, he lit the cigarette and inhaled. That's when he noticed the blood on his hands. He had completely forgotten. Some of the wounds were pretty deep. He tore his T-shirt and constructed a makeshift bandage, covered the cuts, and stopped the bleeding. He winced—there was a sudden throbbing. *I need to go to the hospital.* But he knew he couldn't. *They will know who I am.* He decided to wait a bit longer. He leaned his head on the side of the shed and fell asleep.

He dreamt. In his dream, he was a typical boy with a normal life. His life had been unconventional, an unusual upbringing, one that made him feel like an outcast. Everyone treated him differently. He was teased and called names. He was weird. Odd. Different. He satisfied them and continually acted out and placed himself apart from others. His mohawk, his personal symbol of rebellion and retribution against his father, separated him even further from everyone else.

In his dream, however, his hair was short and neat. He was dressed like any other teenager. The air was thick, as if he were underwater, and he turned slowly, pushing through the heaviness. He saw an ocean, a beautiful, deep-green sea—so green, he didn't think he had ever seen the color in real life. Standing at the water's edge was a girl who looked about his age. She looked at him and smiled. He felt like he knew her. He had met her before. Did she go to his school? The girl walked up to him and took his hand.

She softly caressed his face, leaving a salty spray of sea water on his skin, and whispered, "Remember."

Then she was gone.

He was awakened by a loud crash as the shed doors burst open. Two cops blocked the doorway. He tried to squeeze past them, but they easily grabbed him. He hated being grabbed; he felt trapped, and he struggled to get loose. His injured hand bumped against the door and he screamed.

"Let me go!"

It was futile—they had the upper hand and he couldn't win the battle. His hand was hurting too much. He grudgingly calmed down and resigned himself to being led to the police car.

The cops drove him to the station and questioned him, but he refused to talk at all, to answer any questions. He was still seething with anger. The officers eventually called his parents.

He could tell by the look on his father's face that his father was deeply disappointed in him.

"What happened?" asked his father, sighing and shaking his head.

The boy didn't answer.

They drove to the hospital in silence and the wounds on his hand were stitched and bandaged. As soon as they arrived home, he ran upstairs to his room, slamming the door behind him.

He didn't sleep. He couldn't understand the uncontrollable anger he felt, the need to lash out at everything and everyone. *Why am I so angry? What is wrong with me? I feel so alone.*

He fought to keep the tumultuous emotions away. He began to cry, although he had no idea why he was crying. He was angry, not sad. He immediately stopped the tears, pushed the sadness away. The negative emotions kept trying to sneak through, but he wouldn't let that happen anymore. *I will build a wall. I will stop the feelings from coming. I will end the pain.* He clutched his head and squeezed hard. No more pain, no more fears, no more tears.

BLISS

am obsessed with defining this new connection and can't shake the sense of significant *knowing* that I feel with him. A recognition of the past, a nostalgia. Is he the strange man in my dreams? Since I was a child, I have had the same dream. I don't remember a face. The presence, a figure, embodied and resonated love. And I felt love in return. Each time I had the dream, I wondered—who is this man? I analyzed it, thought about it—was he just a symbol of my desire to have that type of deep love? Had I conjured him up in my subconscious? Would he appear one day? For a long time, I had hoped he would come, because I felt we were somehow destined to be together, fated to meet. However, time and life experiences changed that thought. I had given up hope that he even existed and accepted the possibility that my dreams were just a childhood fantasy, an escape from reality.

Although I don't remember a face in my dreams, only the presence of someone, I do remember dark hair. Although sometimes I'm not even sure whether I completely invented that characteristic as the dreams progressed. The only thing I knew for sure is that a man would enter my life one day, and we would connect in such an astounding, inexplicable way that it would transform the rest of my life. It only seemed logical that it had to be romantic in nature—never would I have expected anything except a happily ever after when this man finally arrived.

This unplanned and unexpected encounter with him turned my cynicism to hope, although I remain confused. There seems to be something larger than us involved in this—there are just too many coincidences. Plus, there is the depth of my emotions, despite the fact that we have only just met. *What faith do I have? What beliefs?* I question this because I'm not a huge believer in destiny, fate, or any kind of divine intervention. I doubted. How could a divine being allow such horrible things to happen in the world? My childhood was not perfect, some parts of my life were painful, and I used to ask God when I was little: *Why me? Why are you allowing these things to happen to me?* As an adult, I finally came to accept the good and bad in my life and appreciated both for what they taught me and how they helped me along my path. I am strong, independent, and confident, and I am in full control of my destiny. Those who live life in victim consciousness can never rise up and succeed. I firmly believe that those who are stuck in unhappiness and wallowing in self-pity are there by choice.

To believe this connection is driven by something divine is too much to completely accept. Free will and perseverance are important, and I won't let myself be at the mercy of fate and some unknown power. However, I am questioning this now. *What are my beliefs and where is this all going? Do I just trust and let go?*

The day after we spent the night together, he sent me a perplexing text.

Him: I just wanted you to know that I am generally monogamous and everything moved too quickly last night. I'm not telling you what to do and it is your prerogative to date and do what you want but I don't operate that way.

What? Is he kidding? I ponder the entire text. His use of the word generally—what does that mean? I laugh but am slightly annoyed. Is he implying that I do this all the time? I think about his words, as I am apt to do with any conversation, and go back and forth trying to decipher any hidden meaning. I decide to let the annoyance go and reply back calmly.

Me: I am not one to sleep around and I understand what you're saying.

Him: OK

That's all he says in response. "OK." *What does that mean?* Does he want to be monogamous? Are we seeing other people? Does he want to see me again? I get confused and start to worry about the definition of our relationship. This is unlike me. I'm usually very balanced. It's too soon to define anything, although I realize part of me wants to define our connection because the intensity is causing me too much confusion. I push those uneasy feelings aside and again, for the second time, I let it go.

The next few weeks are a blur of exhilaration and contentment. We spend a lot of time together, things seem to be moving forward normally, stably. I am happy—more than happy, ecstatic, joyful, peaceful, and extremely comfortable. The feeling of connectedness increases to the point where I begin to miss being with him when we are apart. Not just missing his presence, but I feel like *something* is missing when I am not with him. I chastise myself. I'm in my fifties, so it's not like I'm a naïve teenager falling in love for the first time. I try to rationally analyze everything. But I can't. There is no room for rational thought here. So, I keep going with the flow of whatever is happening.

IV
STAYING ABOVE WATER

DANTE
AND BEATRICE

In that book which is my memory,
On the first page of the chapter that is the day when I first met you,
Appear the words, 'Here begins a new life'.
~ Dante Alighieri, Vita Nuova

Love, that moves the sun and the other stars...
~ Dante Alighieri, Paradiso

Beatrice loved to sit in the garden in the early morning summer hours and listen to the sounds of the birds, watching their hunt for food and listening to the whistling words only they could understand. She would close her eyes and pretend she could understand what they were saying. *Hello! Hello! What's for breakfast? Some worms and some seeds!* She would imagine entire routine conversations amongst the birds.

She also loved to walk the streets of Florence in the early morning, before the heat, before the sun rose too high in the sky and scorched the city. As she strolled, she thought about art. She admired the paintings of the Florentine Cimabue and the Sienese artist Duccio. Her pious upbringing drew her to the paintings of the Madonna. But it was her underlying emotional upheaval that drew her to the emotions the artists infused into their work. The art was about the Madonna, but at a much deeper level it was about spirituality, belief, and the power of God. Beauty and faith. Conflict.

In the midst of her slow, dream-filled walk, she suddenly realized she was late. She rushed back home, fearing she would be late for the May Day party at her house. She still needed to get dressed. In a frenzy, she slipped on an orange dress, one of her favorites, and swept her hair up in a loose bun. *There, now I am ready to greet the guests.*

She hurried downstairs, politely kissed her father on the cheek, and let out a deep sigh of relief.

"Beatrice, sighing like that is not proper. A lady must always be in control and not let loose with emotion like that," chastised her father.

"Yes, father," she replied, politely. *Of course he had to say something like that.* She hardly let loose anything, just a small amount of what she was feeling inside. She wanted to let it all out, be free, tell the world about the Madonna art, the paintings that moved her very deeply. Instead, she stood silently and appropriately beside her father.

The guests trickled in slowly. Beatrice politely kissed their cheeks, behaving like the dutiful daughter that she was supposed to be. Some guests exclaimed that her beauty seemed to increase each time they saw her, others commented on the lovely home, while some praised her father for raising such a respectful daughter.

If only they knew her real self, she thought.

Out of the corner of her eye, Beatrice saw a boy she had never met before. Was he new in town? Surely, she would have heard of him or met him already at many of the other gatherings.

"Ah, Signor Alighieri. How are you this beautiful May Day?" Her father's voice was very welcoming, so there seemed to be some deep friendship there that Beatrice was oblivious to.

"Signor Portinari, we are humbled by your invitation," he politely replied. "My son Dante, my wife…"

"It's a pleasure, Signora. And welcome, Dante; the children will be gathering in the garden. Beatrice, can you take Dante out there, please?" asked her father.

Beatrice wanted to say no, she didn't want to be with the children. They were too immature for her. But she complied and beckoned for Dante to follow her.

Beatrice sensed his eyes on her back as they walked. He had not looked away from her since he arrived.

Beatrice was curious about this boy. For some reason, there was something about him that made her feel uneasy. She couldn't quite place it. It was an uneasiness that was not necessarily negative, just something she had never experienced.

The children played while Beatrice stood and watched. Dante sat on a bench in a corner of the garden by himself. Soon the party was over.

As Dante left, he looked back at Beatrice, who was looking at him. Beatrice thought he looked sad and couldn't imagine why. And then she felt sad. *What is this?* she thought. *He is a stupid, immature boy. Why do I feel sadness about his leaving?* She decided to ignore these feelings and said a polite goodbye as he walked out the door.

They ran into each other twice over the next several years. The first time was brief, and they didn't speak. Beatrice simply wanted to get away from him. Beatrice remembered the meeting, but only with confusion. She couldn't understand why she felt connected to him and at the same time wanted to get away from him. Again, like the previous time they met, she felt his eyes following her as she moved, as if he was trying to memorize her movements. This made her uncomfortable.

The second time was not until nine years later. Beatrice was strolling down a Florentine street, when she recognized Dante. Dante, looking down at the ground and distracted, didn't notice her until she stopped and greeted him. He looked up at her, shocked, and ran in the other direction, mumbling strings of disconnected words under his breath.

"Joy...beauty...must write...Beatrice."

What a strange man, thought Beatrice.

They would see each other again at a wedding—she was there with her husband, and Dante with his wife—and this time, they would actually have a conversation.

Dante saw her from across the room, gathered his courage, and moved towards her.

"Good evening. Beatrice, is that correct?" he asked politely.

She remembered him. The sad boy who stared.

"Signor Dante, I remember you. We played together as children," she remembered.

"Yes, we knew each other as children. Though I don't think we played very much," he corrected. Then he blurted out, "You are beautiful!"

Shocked, Beatrice just stared at him. He then touched her hand softly and she sighed deeply, feeling a sudden wave of recognition, of having known his tenderness. She blushed.

"Dante, why do I know you?"

"Beatrice, you have always known me. I have known you forever," he replied.

"Dante, why do I love you?" she said this without thinking, just words that flew from her lips, words she knew were true.

"Beatrice, you have always loved me. I have loved you forever," he replied.

In that moment, they both knew they were deeply connected, and that nothing could break the bond.

Dante took her hand, pulled her outside to the garden, and impulsively kissed her, touching her shoulder with his hand at the same time.

Beatrice was taken aback, but the moment felt right, and even though they were both married, she did not feel like she was being unfaithful to her husband. Quite the opposite. She felt that by being married she was being unfaithful to Dante.

"Beatrice..." was all Dante could say.

Beatrice felt happiness and sadness all at once, the knowing that something beautiful was beginning, but also sensing sadness because she knew the realistic end. She could sense he felt the same.

Beatrice was overwhelmed with emotion and ran from the garden back to the house. Flushed, faint, and hyperventilating, she wasn't paying attention and ran into her husband, who took one look at her and asked her what was wrong. She looked sick.

"Are you feeling well, Beatrice?" he asked.

"Yes, yes, I am fine. Just not feeling like myself." She wasn't feeling at all like herself. Better than herself, but also worse. "Can we leave please?" she implored.

"Yes, let me get our coats and give our apologies to the hosts," he said with concern.

This was the last time Beatrice and Dante saw each other.

Beatrice died one year later from an illness. As she passed and flowed into the light, her final earthbound thought was of Dante. Her final desire was that they would find each other in death.

When Dante learned of her death, he broke down. He retreated to his writing and began composing poems to her memory. Beatrice influenced all of his writing. She appeared as a character in one of his works that would go on to become an influential piece of literature. He poured his pain into the pages; his anguish upon learning of her death is contained in several poems. In the pages of an important story, he composed a reunion of their souls in heaven—a blissful, spiritual ending to a heartbreaking love in life.

FEARLESS

She was life itself. Wild and free. Wonderfully chaotic.
A perfectly put together mess.
~ The Better Man Project

The yacht screamed over the waves, the wind ripping across the sails, and all on board were holding on for their lives. Except for her. She loved the out-of-control excitement, the anticipation of danger, not knowing what would happen...whether a huge monstrous wave would cross over the bow, maybe even flip the boat, tossing everyone overboard like tiny ants in a massive pond, flailing in the water.

She had changed. She stopped most of her rebellious and self-destructive behaviors and decided to strive for the appearance of perfection. The old, undesirable persona was gone. She was the opposite of that person now and she wanted to live her life to prove to everyone that she was perfect. *Everyone will accept me now; I've changed. I'm perfect and I will get all the love I need.* Sailing for her was part of that, feeling the freedom of the sea and wind. She loved the sea.

As they sailed in the wild sea, she noticed the wind was tinged with a powerful, electric scent, a memory. She recognized the smell; it evoked a remembrance from childhood, but she couldn't recall it clearly. A childhood vision, a dream? She recalled touching the water. And heat and electricity and a message. *The sea spoke to me.* This moment on the ocean brought back that long-ago dream. She felt powerful and connected to the sea, as each little bit of salty spray splashed on her face, making it tingle, like tiny currents of electricity. Each droplet, filled with stirring energy, tried to seep inside her, under her skin, creating an unbroken path from ocean to body. *I burned with that feeling of connectedness. I long for it still. And I remember. Like my dream.*

"Release the jib!" yelled the captain, as he cut across the deck. "You!" He pointed to a boy. "Do it now!"

She jerked out of her trance at the captain's command. The boy was terrified; she saw it in his eyes. He froze. She flew across the boat and grabbed the rope, pulled it, and released the sail before they flipped completely upside down. She laughed loudly and confidently. The wind was still whipping, but once the sails came down, they safely motored into the cove without being thrashed by the waves.

They anchored in a little harbor on an island off the coast of Africa, a two-hour sail from the capital. It was still windy, and getting into the dinghy proved difficult with the waves. When they finally managed to all climb in, they rowed boisterously ashore, excited to eat and drink at the local restaurant.

They ate enough and drank too much, as was the usual routine for the group. They stumbled in the dark to the dinghy, a single flashlight lighting their path, and were shocked to find that it was firmly set in the sand. The tide had receded. They pulled the small boat down to the water's edge, nearly one hundred yards, before they were able to get in and row. However, their progress was thwarted because the little boat could not get very far, as it was barely floating and, in fact, was stuck again in the sand.

"OK, we will have to continue forward," someone said, as they dragged the boat behind them.

However, there was no further. They walked over the wet sand and kept walking, finally reaching the silhouette of the boat in the darkness. It was leaning heavily to the right, obviously no longer floating, wedged deep in the gritty, sandy bottom.

They were literally able to walk the rest of the way to the boat.

They struggled to climb on board because the ladder was too high. After several moments of hectic commotion, and with a little help from each other and the extra adrenaline from too much alcohol, they finally stood on deck.

They played cards late into the night, smoking cigarettes and drinking the last few beers on board. They slept peacefully, drunk and exhausted, waking to a boat surrounded by water.

An adventure at sea, its unpredictability and uncompromising attitude. It is either too wild or too still. *There is no balanced medium and that's how I feel. I am wild and free and sometimes inexplicably stuck. There is no in-between for me.* She was still longing for something more, but just couldn't figure out—what is that something more?

ADRENALINE

Adrenaline is wonderful. It covers pain.
~ Jerry Lewis

"Whoo!! Crazy fuckin' sea!" he yelled, as the water hit him in the face. "Man, this is wild!"

The waves crashed over the deck of the cargo ship, a turbulent sea from a potent storm. The ship, on its way to an "undisclosed" location, carrying weapons and supplies, tore through the sea, pushing its way through the enormous waves, fighting to stay on schedule.

There was an endless supply of alcohol—they had been drinking since breakfast and he was completely drunk. He had no fear, no sense of caution about the sea. He loosely held on to the rail of the ship, his nonchalant attitude in contrast to the danger in his surroundings. The waves poured over him, and he nearly lost his grip several times. He had no fear of death nor of being washed overboard. He felt freedom. Freedom from responsibility, freedom from the pressure of giving others what they want, freedom from surrendering tightly entombed secrets. Freedom from the deep light and dark emotions that were hidden in his soul.

If life could always be like this, I could live without worry, he thought. *I don't fear love because I don't need love. I don't need anything, except this feeling of freedom.*

He was senselessly happy in his boldness. The adrenaline and alcohol drowned out all the confusion and pain even though he logically knew he was simply masking the symptoms. The *why* did not matter at that moment. He only wanted the moment to last as long as possible. He didn't want to go home, he didn't want to go back to combat—he just wanted to remain on the deck of this ship for the rest of his life. Escaping everything.

Suddenly, a huge wave swept over the stern of the ship and battered him so hard he lost his grip on the railing and flew backwards. He tried to grasp at something, anything to keep from being thrown overboard, but there wasn't anything to grab onto. He was engulfed in water. The exhilaration suddenly turned to terror, as he realized there was nothing to prevent him from being thrown into the sea. There was nothing he could do; he simply surrendered. He did not believe in God. However, he suddenly whispered a prayer, a plea for help, asking for a merciful and quick death.

He was gasping for breath and blinded by the water, when he felt a hand firmly grasp his wrist and stop his uncontrollable plummet. He was pulled forward toward the railing, and he reached out, clasping his arms around the life preserver clipped to the rail. He was safe. He dragged himself toward the door, soaking wet and shaking from cold and fear. He was hyperventilating, and the incredible, drunken, adrenaline rush had morphed into a sobering realization of just how close he had come to death. He couldn't breathe. His friends rushed toward him, laughing and only mildly concerned for his safety. They were still too drunk to realize the potential disaster that had been averted. He was, however, completely lucid.

"Hey, who grabbed me?" he asked.

"Grabbed you? Nobody—you were out there all by yourself," one of them answered.

"Well, someone grabbed me and stopped me from going overboard."

"Dude, you were alone out there. Maybe it was God!" one joked.

Alone? He was confused. Someone definitely grabbed him and saved his life. Not God. He controlled his own life and God did not exist.

That night, he dreamt of a woman who rose from the ocean and held out her hand to him. She was ethereally beautiful. She was wearing a long, tangerine-colored robe; her long blonde hair was loose and flowing wildly in the wind. She asked him to take her hand, to trust her, but he was fearful, so he turned his back and walked away. The woman stood there smiling.

"One day," she whispered confidently.

WALLS

Things are going so well between us. *Perfectly*. Although I am learning that perfection is a state that can never be truly attained. We can aim for perfection, but can we truly ever reach it? It can be used to set goals perhaps, but it will always disappoint. I notice how I just used the term *perfectly*, despite my recent discoveries about perfection. Does my usage mean anything? As usual, I am over-analyzing my thoughts, words, behaviors...time to let that go and not worry and stop thinking that everything has a secret meaning behind it. *Relax*.

I'm on my way to meet him for a walk along the river, one of my favorite spots. The anticipation and excitement I feel about seeing him makes my stomach jump and my face tingle...so strange. It's only been a few days since I saw him last. Why do I want to see him so badly? *You're in love, stupid.*

"Why 'stupid'?" I say aloud.

It's too soon.

"Well, I won't tell him how I feel, of course," I say aloud to myself.

Does he love you back?

"Yes!" I say.

Are you sure about that?

"Stop. Those are my fears talking. Stop!" I yell.

I stop. I am not only arguing with myself in my head, but apparently out loud, since several people have turned and looked at me. Of course, I won't tell him how I feel. Not now. I know he loves me. I can't explain how I know, it's just a knowing. I think it's just part of the connectedness we share. I know he loves me. We just haven't said it yet. It's not time. I feel like a swooning, out-of-control idiot at times. I sound incredibly naïve, as if I am experiencing love for the first time, and this bothers me. I feel like I'm reading my diary from my teen years. My mind races to think things through. Am I feeling too much? Am I thinking too much? I feel off-balance—but in a giddy sort of way. This concerns me a bit. I rely on my intuition to make decisions and usually am pretty certain when I've made the "right" choice. I am hesitating. There is something tapping, trying to get in, reminding me of something. It's not a bad feeling—it's more a feeling of not seeing something I need to see. Am I missing something? I dismiss it. It's probably just butterflies.

The hike is beautiful; the leaves are just starting to change, autumn is coming, and the day is warm enough that I don't need a jacket. Brilliant sunshine. We hold hands. I smile to myself and think: *this is perfect.*

We sit on an old log near our cars after our walk, laughing about some silly joke. I'm simply enjoying the moment. *I wish this could last longer.* He suddenly looks at his watch and gets up, saying he needs to go soon. What? I'm confused. I thought he was free the rest of the day. There is a sudden shift, an alarm goes off.

Warning Warning! Something is wrong. As he speaks, I think to myself that he's lying. How would I know? And he is an honest, kind person...but I sense that there is something he isn't telling me. It's not his body language or any other physical signal—it's like a whisper in my head. And that whisper is saying he doesn't want to be with me, he *wants* to leave. I don't say a word though.

As I drive away, I sense it again—distancing, like something is blocking the free flow of emotions. I clearly see a picture of a wall. I have no idea what that means though. All I am focusing on right now is the fact that I am suddenly feeling overwhelmed with sadness, hopelessness, and fear. I feel insecure and needy, emotions I have not felt in many years. *I am confident! How are these emotions overpowering me? Everything is fine,* I tell myself. *Stop getting stuck in your head about this!* So unlike me to have these thoughts popping into my head out of nowhere. However, I can't shake the feeling. I go home and try to make it go away, try to bury it deep inside, try to erase it, as is my usual response to bothersome feelings. I'm the queen of hiding her negative emotions. The queen of perfection. But I am unsuccessful and the feeling that something bad is coming lingers and permeates the rest of my day.

I bring up the feelings when we talk the next day. As much as I want to let this go and avoid conflict, it's just bothering me way too much. I explain my feelings of dread, fear, hopelessness. And the sudden distance, the very clear picture of the wall.

"This is really strange and I'm wondering why I sensed this," I say.

He's silent for a moment, looks down at his hands, obviously uncomfortable, and takes a deep breath.

He then confesses (and it felt like a confession, like he had never told anyone else about this "deep, dark secret") that he has an issue about opening up and letting people in. Vulnerability. Over the years, he has built "walls."

Strange, I saw those walls.

"Why?" I ask, already knowing the answer. Walls protect, hide, and we all do this to some extent.

This prevents him from letting things out, as well as letting things in, he says casually, with a smile, although I sense an underlying unease. I think, *what things? Emotions.* I let him continue. He laid each brick year after year, experience after experience, and the wall can't come down; it is indestructible. His face is serious now and the words come out awkwardly.

This is completely baffling to me because not once since I've met him have I felt any walls. I have sensed quite the opposite. He has been free with his thoughts and emotions (except for yesterday). But as the conversation continues, and I ask several very pointed questions about his walls, I feel the distance growing, the connection fading. I question what I'm feeling. Are these just my own fears and insecurities coming out, sensing things that I cannot possibly sense? I need more information.

Why don't you just tear the walls down?

"I can't tear the walls down," he says.

Wait. I didn't ask that out loud.

"Maybe you don't *want* them to come down," I tell him. "You're protecting yourself, keeping yourself from feeling pain."

I'm so smart, armchair psychologist, I can fix this.

He doesn't reply, and since we both have things to do, the conversation ends.

I'm not crazy about this new discovery. I feel things slipping even further into murkiness, out of my control. I have no idea what to do or what this all means. Another red flag? I dismiss it. My love will set him free. *Right. Just like every other woman who thinks she can change a man.*

That night I have a vivid, intense dream. I am back on my island, my home, with my sister, walking on a familiar street. A man with a bar apron opens a door, looks right at me, and shouts:

"Remember these numbers! 12, 15, 18, 20, 22." He repeats the numbers again, saying, "Don't forget. Remember these numbers." He slams the door shut.

Then he opens the door again and says, "Oh, and the number 3!"

The door closes and I wake up.

I am perplexed by my dream but obediently write down the numbers. I have no idea what they mean. They appear meaningless and are not connected to anything in my life. But I was told to remember them. Lottery numbers? Hmmmm. A psychic dream so I can win the lottery? Well, five numbers plus the Powerball, those are my numbers. *Maybe I'll play Powerball this week!* I feel though, that these numbers have a much deeper mystical meaning.

We seem to easily flow back into seeing each other after our talk, experiencing moments of intense connectedness, just talking or being or doing whatever we end up doing, living in the moment. As the week goes by, I feel comfortable, confident, at peace. I am shocked, impressed, awed, and completely in love. And I will not let this slip away.

V

DESOLATION

SHAH JAHAN AND MUMTAZ MAHAL

There is something in love, otherwise the Taj Mahal
wouldn't have been built on a corpse.
~ Janhangir Hussain

Because we as humans, the vessels of love,
are fragile in our existence.
~ Farhan Shajahan

S hah Jahan was strolling down the Meena Bazaar, when he caught a glimpse of a girl selling silk and glass beads. It was love at first sight. Her beauty surpassed that of any woman he had ever seen, and he felt an instant connection. She looked up from her beads and silk and looked into his eyes, like she was looking right through to his soul. He wanted to speak with her, but his courtiers urged him to keep moving, so he simply smiled at her in greeting. The girl smiled back. In her deep brown eyes, he saw love. *She loves me*, he thought. He knew he wanted to marry her.

"Find out who that girl is," Jahan ordered, pointing in her direction.

Arjumand. *A beautiful name for the most beautiful woman*, he thought, when he learned her name. He was possessed and driven. *We must be together*. The marriage was arranged.

They impatiently longed for each other, as it would be five years before they were finally married. As was the custom, he took another wife in the meantime, but he hungered for the day when he would marry his true love. She told him his other marriages did not bother her. Their love was powerful, and she knew he had no feelings for his other wives.

During those years of waiting, he would visit her often at her home in the company of a chaperone. They would stare at each other, sometimes barely speaking, fighting the desire to reach out and make physical contact. The magnetism in the attraction kept them suspended and they would lose track of time. When they parted, sorrow filled the gaps in the air. The sorrow would linger until they were both together again.

"I see you," he said one day. "I know you like I know myself."

She nodded, understanding completely what he meant. That energetic knowledge seemed to surround them.

Finally, the day of the wedding arrived. When they both were finally able to touch one another, it was like an explosion of energy. As their bodies moved together, there was a familiarity, a definitive and deep connection. When he first entered her, they shared a vision of stars, the sea, and a cross. An intense explosion of light. They saw visions of themselves in familiar places somewhere in time, although neither had any memory in this life of those places. They moved together in love, their bodies feeling the utter serenity and passion of their connected souls. Never had Jahan ever felt this feeling, the intensity, the beauty of lovemaking. Arjumand, never having experience in bodily pleasures, did not know what to expect, but it was even more pleasurable than her imagination had ever envisioned. They came together, in a blinding light, knowing they were meant to be.

He bestowed upon her a new name: Mumtaz Mahal, which meant "Jewel of the Palace." Although he already had other wives, he treasured her above all and she was the sole recipient of his true love. They had a very deep and loving marriage. Poets would extol her beauty, gracefulness, and compassion. She was his trusted companion and traveled with him all over the Mughal Empire. The intimacy, deep affection, and favor which he felt for Mumtaz exceeded all of what he felt for any other.

The years passed and they had several children. They were happy and looked forward to many years together.

"Mumtaz, I cannot imagine life without you," he told her one day, as he rubbed her very pregnant belly.

"It is the same for me. I am so happy you visited the bazaar that day. It seems like yesterday that I saw your smile," she replied.

"I will love you forever," he vowed passionately.

However, their joyous life together would come to an end sooner than expected. Unexpectedly, during the birth of their child, Mumtaz began bleeding uncontrollably. The bleeding could not be stopped—there was nothing to be done. Jahan held her hand, praying that her life be spared. His tears fell upon her face and she opened her eyes,

"I will see you soon," she whispered, taking one final breath and releasing a sigh as her soul escaped through her lips.

Jahan was utterly heartbroken. He could not understand why the gods took his Mumtaz from him so soon. They were happy. He was paralyzed with grief—his pain so immense, he was inconsolable. How would he live the rest of his life without her?

His pain and grief inspired him to build a monument to his love, his light, his eternal soulmate. She would always be remembered. Jahan spent almost all of his vast fortune and invested years of his time constructing a monument to honor Mumtaz. Her body was eventually interred in the monument, the Taj Mahal, as was his, when he finally joined her in the afterlife.

LOVE LESSONS

The most painful thing is losing yourself in the process of loving someone too much, and forgetting that you are special too.
~ Ernest Hemingway

Heartbreak. *I love him beyond words. We were supposed to get married.* He proposed, she said yes, then her parents balked. She was only a sophomore in college. Too young, too much life to live to get married so soon. So, she told him no after she had already told him yes. That was the beginning of the end, or maybe it was already going to end, and this was the catalyst. A few months later, after some fierce arguments, he told her it was over. No. She needed him. She was attached to him, way more than she should have been, but she didn't see that then. She felt lost, like losing him she was losing everything, losing herself. She was alone in a strange place, having moved to be with him. Never really made her own friends, never really had her own life. Dependent on him for everything.

This seemed worse than any pain she had experienced. She felt abandoned, rejected, and alone. Her stepfather, who she loved like he was her real father, wrote her a letter, reminding her that who she became and what she blossomed into because of that relationship was not lost. This was always within her: the fearlessness, the confidence, the desire and ability to give so much love. The love just helped bring these things out into the world. She would find someone else one day who would appreciate those qualities, and she would be loved as deeply in return. That would be a profound love. It wasn't until thirty years later, when she read the letter again after her stepfather's death and in the midst of emotional and spiritual chaos, that she really heard the words and finally understood what he meant.

It took a long time for her to finally get over him. She spent many years thinking back on the relationship and their connection, wondering what she had done wrong, how she could have fixed things. She would become emotionally guarded and only half present in her life. There were no leaps of faith, just practical decisions that would help her protect herself and live what she thought was an emotionally balanced life.

He would often appear in her dreams; although she never saw his face, she assumed it was him. Just a bright silhouette, full of love and acceptance. The dreams always ended with him abandoning her or a series of unusual circumstances kept them apart. It didn't consume her nor take over her life, but it was there in the background, a nagging feeling of unfinished business. Eventually, she realized the toxicity of the attachment and accepted the need to release the connection. There was a lesson to be learned—that was the reason for his coming into her life. Everything we experience teaches us something important and builds our strength.

She had grown so much since then and was finally a strong and independent woman. Back then, she was a needy, clinging fool.

A lesson learned. However, she was wrong about the lesson—she understood the lesson to mean that she should not build deep attachments to anyone. Emotionally, all she needed was herself. And she would continue to live this way until her life was again turned upside down.

FORTIFICATION

There are four kinds of people in the world, Ms. Harper. Those who build walls. Those who protect walls. Those who breach walls. And those who tear down walls. Much of life is discovering who you are. When you find out, you also realize there are places you can no longer go, things you can no longer do, words you can no longer say.
~ P.S. Baber, Cassie Draws the Universe

He wasn't sure what he wanted to do. He was leaving the next day, off to boot camp. He had a confusing fear growing in him, something he couldn't quite understand. It wasn't tied to anything in particular...just a general apprehension. *Ridiculous.* He pushed it away.

He made the phone call around one a.m. from a payphone around the corner from the bar. She said yes. He knew she would. She knew he was completely trashed, but it didn't matter. Always impulsive about certain things, he was all in. His decision was a contradiction in many ways, although he didn't realize it at the time. He felt love, but it was muted. As if only a part of him was present, while the truly emotional, deep soul portion was completely hidden. He refused to acknowledge the doubt and fear until much later. His fear of being alone, without a woman, a companion, someone to help pass the time, was far stronger.

Everything about his life was based in spontaneity. All of his decisions were fearless and fast. If he kept going forward at lightning speed, nothing could hurt him. Keep moving, don't stop.

When the end came, he was only slightly surprised. He was never home, always somewhere overseas, months, years at a time. The end came quickly and impersonally in a letter. It was done. He wasn't heartbroken. Yes, there were feelings of regret, but he simply shrugged his shoulders and thought, *Oh well*. He didn't try to fix things, repair the damage. Because inside he felt free, released. He was more peaceful alone. And freer, not having to satisfy others' needs, feeling the constant pressure of their emotional desires. It was too intense and overwhelming; alone, he was protected and liberated.

Defiantly, he added another brick to his wall, closing himself off further from feeling any pain. Ironically, it would also prevent him from feeling authentic joy. The walls had grown slowly over time without him even realizing how high they had become. They had grown to his waist, surrounding him and protecting him from pain and successfully keeping others at a distance. Always alone emotionally, always safe. More bricks were laid upon each other as time passed. War, heartbreak, death, and loss. Too many bricks—he lost count—and soon the wall was above his head. Nobody could tear it down, the immense towering fort, until it finally reached the point where he was helpless, believing he was trapped inside and unable to climb out or knock the wall down.

REJECTION

I am just flowing with everything. Not thinking, living in the moment: work, friends, hobbies, and, of course, him. Although we haven't spent a lot of time together, we have had moments of deep, intense connectedness that stay with me. I close my eyes and can imagine those moments so clearly. So beautiful, they almost seem like fantasy. I tell myself I am living in the moment, yet at times I feel I'm not in the present. I feel a nostalgic pull to the past...a past time? A feeling of knowing him a long time ago. However, it feels so perfectly aligned to the moment, as if this is how it was always meant to be. These are very strange and obscure feelings that leave me ecstatic, but at the same time bewildered. I keep trying to make sense of these feelings and their significance, searching for answers within myself.

There is an intense, profound bond in our lovemaking that night. That night is so prominent in my memory. I vividly remember all the mystical and physical sensations. The feel of our bodies moving together, the overwhelming intensity, and my own amazement at the experience. Mystical, because the experience was transcendental, something that was beyond pure emotion. Whatever this connection is, it is profound, and I need to assign it a meaning. As if assigning a meaning would make it more plausible.

I didn't see it coming. By the end of the next day, I sense the damn distance creeping in again. I hadn't even seen him, nor did we talk the entire day. I'm walking alone along the river and see a stone wall and I stop. The wall. His walls are up. *Are these simply my fears of rejection and abandonment? Fear of being hurt? Am I reacting because of my fears?* No, I know beyond a doubt he is distancing himself. It's not me. I feel confident and clear-headed. It's him. There is a certainty in my intuition—what I am sensing are his feelings. I know I'm right, as crazy as it sounds.

I immediately text him and ask if I can see him this evening.

I'm terrified. I don't know what I'm going to say. For the first time in a long time, I have no prepared speech and I'm not in control of my emotions or the words that are about to come out of my mouth. I'm scared to expose myself, scared to tell him how I feel. Fear of rejection, fear of pain. But also there is a bravery that comes out of nowhere, something completely alien to me, that propels me to be vulnerable. So I tell him the truth.

Surprisingly, he doesn't question what I tell him about my intuition. Not so surprisingly, the first thing he says is that his walls are up. This time I ask more questions.

"Why don't you just tear the walls down?" I ask.

"I can't; they have been there too long. They are massive and solid," he answers, in a matter-of-fact tone. A little cold, actually.

"Have you tried to tear them down? Are you sure that you aren't just afraid to tear them down? What's on the other side?" I ask in quick-fire succession.

He doesn't reply—just sits there. Then he slowly starts to explain, carefully and hesitantly, all the while looking the other way. I can tell this is difficult for him. I can feel his pain as he answers my questions. His pain is my pain. Each word he speaks becomes a part of my own emotions. This scares me. I've always thought I was a bit empathic, but this is the first time I have clearly noticed that I can feel and relate to others' emotions.

He says the walls are permanent. They are not coming down because he doesn't want them to come down. It's too much and too intense, so it's better to keep them up and live his life. He cannot and does not want to love. His words destroy my hope. If someone purposefully does not want to let their guard down, then there is nothing that can be done until that person recognizes walls are a hindrance. I can't understand how anyone can live like this—not enjoying each moment in life, keeping others out and protecting yourself from all things, pain *and* love.

What I want from him is on the other side of the wall. I want those moments back, when I was able to glimpse through the cracks in the wall. I realize that no matter how hard I try to fix this, I can't. This is out of my control. Those moments we shared are lost.

I lose control. For the first time in a long time, I can't control the tears that start to pool in my eyes. I really don't want to cry—I don't want to show my weakness, my vulnerability, my pain, my need. But there they are, those not-so-perfect emotions, clearly visible for him to see. I don't say that I love him, I don't speak the words. I try to explain my feelings without using *those* words. However, it's pretty clear how I feel. And I cry. Dammit. I cry and I don't want to. It's over.

Not once during the conversation did he actually say he didn't want to see me again. In fact, despite his walls and the surrounding emotions, it seems clear that he wants us to continue as we are—to continue on in a relationship where one person feels love and the other is apathetic and eager to run at every moment. *Why would I want that?* I tell him I'm not sure I can do this without reciprocating feelings (again, never saying the word love). I am feeling way too vulnerable for that.

"I'm not ready for love," he whispers.

I feel like I've been pierced in the heart. Even though I understood his pain, his need for the walls, all I can feel is my own pain now. This is done. *How could I have been wrong about this?* I felt his love. There are no doubts in my heart *and* mind, despite his words of rejection. I sensed it. There is no denying it, no matter what he claims. This is what would keep me going through the rest of my journey, my belief that our love for each other would bring down the walls.

We talked a lot that night. At one point, I almost left to go home, but I decided to stay. I am such a live-in-the-moment person, there was no way I was going to give up having what was possibly a last night with him, whether he thought he loved me or not. We made love, but it was different. I felt the gap in the distance widening.

The next morning, there was no denying the chasm between us; he had drifted farther away. We went for a hike. I was very quiet, pretending to be pensive, but seething inside. Angry at him for not loving me. No, for not *wanting* to love me. As if anyone has control over loving someone. Either you do or you don't... and if you want to walk away regardless, then that's your choice. But denying it? That was annoying and stupid and flippant. What was worse was that I had no control over anything... I wish I did. Me, the controller and fixer. I don't know how to fix this.

I went home completely crushed. Although we didn't talk about it after last night, I knew it was over. I decide to let him be, give him space, let him figure out what he wants. I live my life...sort of.

My primal fears kick in. I begin to worry, to fear, to deeply feel the hurt, to wonder what is going on in his mind. I am desperate, insane almost. I try to bury him, forget about him, erase the pain, the memory... This is not like me—why am I so consumed with this? I usually bounce back so easily from these things. I reach out to him two more times over the weekend, seeing if he is free to get together. Again desperation, grasping for straws. A need. He finally replies, saying he's tired. Again, the disappointment, the feeling of abandonment, like he's preparing to leave—or has he already left? Am I in denial? He is going, if not gone already.

Finally, clarity, although not what I wanted. He basically breaks up with me via text. My first text break-up. After all of our long conversations, moments of intimacy, and honest words, he sends me a *text* saying we should just be friends...not ready for love, too many walls...all the same things he said before. We have a long virtual conversation, filled with thought-provoking back-and-forth words, which soon exhausts me. He is trying to act kind, like he doesn't want to hurt me. Or is he just trying to lessen his guilt? I can't tell. His words are sincere. I feel that.

Him: The speed of our entanglement coupled with the stress in my life right now makes it too hard to delve deeper. This is heading to a place I'm not ready to go right now.

Blunt, painful words...and the walls...the ever-present walls that he continues to claim cannot come down—of course, he mentions those fucking walls again. I hate those walls.

I am understanding and respond very logically and calmly, even though inside I want to yell, scream, shake him.

Me: I probably shouldn't have completely told you how I felt that day, but I knew it would have nagged at me and would have eventually been our undoing anyway. It was a lose-lose decision for me, and I knew that. This is all unexpected for me too.

I never thought I would fall in out-of-control love like this, I think to myself.

I reply through my tears.

Me: Sure, let's be friends

Writing lies, feeling truths.

He says a bit more, about how it's been troubling him for days and he thinks we are searching for something similar, but the timing and depth aren't well suited. He doesn't want to completely disconnect but wants to share his perspective. I'm still keeping my cool, still set on replying logically and rationally. So just friends.

Me: Just friends then?

Him: Romantic is scary with the speed it occurred.

Me: You say that like love gives you a choice. Ha. Anyway, I really do understand. I think we just don't see each other, let things normalize. See what happens later, if anything. That's really the only solution.

Him: OK

Him: Normalize.

Me: Wrong word. I mean back to before we met. I guess that's really for me. It's been a whirlwind and there are emotions and I need to just get grounded.

Him: Yeah, you and me both.

Me: I think I'm going to sleep. So goodnight. Goodbye? I don't know what to say. But I will put a string of clichés together. I believe them even though they are cheesy. Everything happens for a reason, if something is meant to be it will happen, and you just have to have faith that everything will work out. I'm way too positive sometimes. I know you will be fine and get past the stresses in your life right now. But in the moment, hard to see that, I know.

Him: Thank you. I hope it's not goodbye but not sure how to step thru differing points of view. I have a problem with faith and trust and that comes from a place long, long before you, or anyone, for that matter. That said, all is well and hope we can keep close in touch. You have an unbelievable beautiful spirit to share with someone less walled up.

I don't reply. I let it go. I don't know what else to say. His words are beautiful, but their beauty only hurts me more. I wish he could have been an asshole instead. I replied very calmly, very rationally through the entire conversation, so unlike how I was really feeling. Devasted. Upset. Angry. We are done. I have to let him go now. Goodbye.

VI

AWAKENING FAITH

JFK & MARILYN

I believe that everything happens for a reason.
People change so that you can learn to let go.
Things go wrong so that you appreciate them when they're right.
~ Marilyn Monroe

"Do people always fall in love with things they can't have?"
"Always," Carol said, smiling too.
~ Patricia Highsmith, The Price of Salt

t was April 1957. Senator John F. Kennedy was attending dinner in New York City with his wife, Jacqueline. It was close to the end of the evening, and he was tired from speeches, interviews, and other endless engagements. It didn't help that he wasn't perfectly healthy. His back hurt a lot some days and, although he felt he could hardly move, he never let anyone in the public know. No one else except close family and his doctors knew he suffered from "ill health," and his quiet stoicism (and those who were good at hiding carefully guarded family secrets) prevented anyone from finding out. His last serious episode had been in January, when he had been hospitalized for several days. Although he was never "normal," he was feeling better than usual today.

He sat at the table, making small talk with several other attendees. There was something happening at the other end of the room. He looked up and saw a stunning blonde woman surrounded by several people. Her beauty was more than just physical. He felt her waves of energy and sexuality from across the room. He recognized her. Marilyn Monroe. She turned her head as if she sensed his eyes were on her. She glanced at him and smiled. He smiled back and waved.

Later that evening, Marilyn was walking to the powder room to freshen up when she felt as if she was being intently watched; she peered over her shoulder. She was instantly captivated. That same man she had seen earlier, with the gorgeous smile and friendly wave, was looking straight at her. It was a couple of seconds before she realized it was Jack Kennedy. She continued smiling as she walked past, but she didn't stop to talk to him. But she would remember that moment. That was the moment she fell in love. He stood up and came toward her, but her husband had already taken her arm and led her away, leaving Jack standing, staring at her. She smiled and waved. He smiled and shrugged.

They would meet again four years later at a dinner party. Jack was now the newly elected President of the United States. They were surrounded by fans and supporters who wanted their full attention, but the instant they saw each other, they ignored everyone around them and moved toward one another

"Ms. Monroe," said Jack.

"Mr. President," smiled Marilyn. "Please, call me Marilyn."

"Call me Jack, but only when nobody is around!" he said under his breath, and then he winked at her.

As their hands reached toward one another to politely shake hands, they felt the heat radiating from their fingertips, until finally their hands touched, and centuries of memories came flooding back, hitting them with tremendous recognition, each molecule sensing the other as a long-lost counterpart.

"It's you," said Marilyn, surprised.

"Yes, it's me!" teased Jack, not understanding quite what she was saying.

Marilyn knew that he was the *one* she was meant to be with, the *one* she had known through the ages, the light that shared her soul with her in the past, the *one* that made her complete. The pieces of the puzzle came together, and she thought, *I am home.* She was happy, but also sad, because he was the President of the United States, he was married, and realistically there was no possibility for them to be together. They went their separate ways the rest of the night, occupied in conversation with fans and supporters.

It was several months until they saw each other again at the home of a famous Hollywood star, on Jack's birthday. Marilyn couldn't wait to see him and hoped they could have a longer conversation this time. She finally saw him in a doorway, talking with a man she didn't recognize. Crazy butterflies in her stomach. She wondered what he thought of her.

If she could have read his mind, she would have learned that he couldn't shake the desire to be with her. There was a powerful attraction. She was on his mind constantly since he last saw her. Always lurking in the background though, was the knowledge that they could never be together, at least while he was President. Maybe after? But divorce? That would never happen. He would be finished. *But she was worth it. She was more than worth it.*

When he saw her that night, ethereally beautiful with her dazzling energy, he was stirred even more. She had a radiance, a magical light, mystery. She seemed not of this world. And there she stood. Marilyn. She smiled at him and nodded her head in the direction of the stairs and walked away. He excused himself, saying he needed to use the restroom, the Secret Service right behind him.

"Stop, I can go to the bathroom by myself. I don't need you following me," he commanded.

He went up the stairs to find several doors—in fact, many doors. He wasn't sure where she was, so he simply began to open doors. As he was opening door number two (door number one was a child's room), he heard a sound down the hall.

"Come on!" urged Marilyn.

As he was about to follow her, one of his Secret Service agents came up behind him.

"Mr. President, is everything OK?" the agent asked, looking around.

"Discretion and privacy please," said Jack, as he walked into the room, and shut the door behind him.

"I so want you!" he whispered, as he kissed her softly on her neck.

"And I you, Mr. President," she teased, wrapping her arms around him.

He softly kissed her lips, then her neck again, moving lower until he kissed the top of her breast. Electric.

She sighed, and turned her back to him. "Unzip me."

He slowly pulled her zipper down.

"Hurry," she begged. "I want you inside me."

She was aching for him. Her dress slid down to the floor and she faced him, quickly helping him get undressed. They uninhibitedly groped each other in fiery passion and fell back on the bed. She hurriedly guided him inside her. It was hot and impatient sex.

When it was done, they both laid back, satisfied. No, nourished.

"I feel so connected to you..." she panted, still recovering. "I don't understand. Almost like when you are inside me, you are...me."

"Marilyn, I love you."

She was shocked by his words, and she could tell he was equally shocked to have said them. *But they are true.*

They gazed at one another, their eyes acutely perceiving the truth that existed clearly in their souls. A sudden sadness permeated the air between them. This was perhaps a one-time thing. They could never truly be together, and spending time alone again would likely be impossible. He would give up anything for her. But they knew the reality.

Marilyn cried. He gently wiped away her tears.

"It'll be OK. We'll make it work somehow." He tenderly caressed her cheek, reassuring her, but in his mind, he knew it would never work.

They dressed and discreetly slipped downstairs, one at a time. Nobody noticed their return amid the raucous laughter and copious drinking. They sat at opposite ends of the table, occasionally glancing at each other until the night ended.

As Jack was leaving, he announced loudly, "Marilyn, I would like you to sing 'Happy Birthday' to me at my celebration tonight. Would you do me the honor?"

Shocked, Marilyn replied, "Why, of course, Mr. President."

Jack, Jack, Jack. Yes, I will sing "Happy Birthday" to you, from the stage, while you sit with your wife and family.

"Five minutes, Ms. Monroe," announced the stage manager.

She looked at herself in the mirror in the dressing room. *I look awful.* She felt hopeless and heartbroken, understanding how deeply in love she was with Jack and realizing that they could not be together. *Time for another pill.* She shakily opened a prescription bottle. Several pills fell into her hand, and she swallowed them all. *I need to get it together. Need to be happy. Erase the damn sadness.* She struggled to regain her balance and purge her emotions. Too much had happened this week and she was on the verge of being kicked off the movie set. Life was a chaotic disaster right now. She pulled herself together and walked on to the stage.

"Happy birthday, Mr. President... Happy birthday to you!" sang Marilyn, as she finished the song.

In drug-induced spontaneity, she announced she would sing another song. She quickly and clumsily jumped into "Thanks for the Memory." She wanted him to know that he meant something more to her, that it was not just a fuck, and that she would always think of him. She needed him to understand. Her mind was spinning—her emotions were a swirl of loss and pain. She sensed she would never see him again.

She sang, but changed the lyrics in her head:

Jack, thank you.
For the things you've done
The love that we've won
The way you touch me
But I feel we are undone
I have to set myself free.

This was the last time they saw each other. Marilyn quickly fell into a deep depression and took her own life a short time later. She swallowed several bottles of various pills and unsuccessfully attempted to make a phone call to Jack; she wanted to say goodbye. Her sorrow in her life, her fears, and tumultuous emotions were too immense. The love she felt for Jack was too great and she didn't want to be alone without him. She set herself free and she set Jack free, so he would no longer hunger for the opportunity to be with her. His desire would always remain though, and he was devastated when he heard about her death. Shortly after her death, he was assassinated and departed to the light, to join Marilyn. They both would be reborn a few years later, in what was likely to be their final incarnation on Earth.

ADRIFT WITHOUT AN ANCHOR

A boat in the ocean
adrift, directionless
Without a rudder
Or an anchor
I am lost
Searching for land
But not knowing
What it looks like
~ Manish Mohan

Her stepfather. Her father. He was her real father. He was the family anchor. He was *her* anchor. The stable, logical, and clear man who everyone sought out for advice. His death brought a deep shock. Even though he had incurable cancer and death was always inevitable, she had wished for a miracle. That he would heal, recover, and live. Her family was special—cancer, death didn't happen to them. It was something that happened to other people. They were lucky and blessed. But there was his body, frail, sickly, empty. His soul was gone, and the wonderful man that he was, was no longer there. She didn't cry deeply right away, just a few tears. Her mother and sister were there, her mother devastated. She made phone calls and arrangements, moving in slow motion, in a dream state that was slowly turning into a nightmare.

Time passed and the pain lessened, although there was still an ache in her heart—"saudades," a Portuguese word that does not have a literal translation in English, but close to meaning a heartfelt nostalgic longing for someone or for a place. This longing evokes a bittersweet desire for that one thing that is irreplaceable. Memories are all that she has left now along with a perpetual sense of being lost, not knowing which path to take nor which choice to make.

With his death came a realization of her own unhappiness. A lack of fulfillment, an unknown feeling that her life was meant to be something more than what it was right now. She was unhappy and felt stuck in her marriage. She lacked a driving passion for something...anything. She had no idea what the something was, but she sensed a lack of significance in her everyday existence. What she thought was a perfect life was really an illusion. Her time was spent doing absolutely everything for everyone else and very little for herself. She wondered if this was simply a mid-life crisis, a sudden acknowledgment that her life was half over and she was running out of time to do something important?

She felt something deeper than that and, in that moment, made a drastic but necessary decision: She asked her husband for a divorce. It was something she had promised herself she would never do. It wasn't an easy choice—she wanted to preserve the perfect life she created, keep her children secure, and continue to let the outside world think she was still "perfect." It was, after all, easier to continue on the path of security than to venture off on her own into the unknown.

With difficulty, but with resolution, she made her decision and moved out. She wanted and needed something new, a new home with her own energy, a new life. And so it began. The pursuit of inner knowledge, as well as creation of something that was just hers, would take time. What was her passion? What work could she do to make some income and yet create authenticity and bring meaning to her life? Who the hell was she? She clung to the letter her father had written her many years ago, his wise words that gave her strength. She folded it neatly and it remained in her nightstand drawer as a reminder of her strength.

AN UNFORGIVEN
DEATH

Forgiveness doesn't excuse their behavior;
Forgiveness prevents their behavior from destroying your heart.
~ Unknown

There was no forgiveness. Although his father passed peacefully and quickly, he had wanted a mutual forgiveness of all past disagreements. They never had the chance to speak, after the anger and harsh words. Their religious beliefs did not align. His father's devout religious beliefs and his own refusal to believe in anything beyond the logical, physical, earthbound existence would sustain the deep conflict in their relationship. He was and always would be the prodigal son, without faith, without a belief that there was something bigger than himself.

The pain was more than just the loss of a person—it was the inability to realize final closure, to forgive and be forgiven, including the need to forgive himself. The wound was open, and he slowly sealed the breach in his wall with additional bricks. One by one, he slid them into place, blocking out not only the pain, but also the love. This was purposeful; he knew exactly what he was doing. Why feel anything at all, if in the end, there was only pain? His self-protection would only serve to make things worse, but he moved on, not caring if he was imprisoned and had closed everyone else out. He was OK being alone.

All he had left was a letter from his father, expressing his disappointment in his son. It was an angry, hateful letter, disavowing and rejecting his son. He reacted to his father's letter and his death by throwing more bricks on top of his wall, until he had a roof over his head, a construct of his own making. Keep the pain away. He wouldn't open his heart to anyone. With anger and bitterness, which he heaved over the walls before they closed in on him, he would keep that letter for a very long time.

On the other side of the wall, a storm brewed. Emotions churned, demanding freedom, yearning to return home. This was wrong. The emotions, cut off from their source, were building to a point of explosion. Nowhere to go. They belonged to him; they felt the pull to return to him. The pressure was building. His higher self, his soul, was in torment trapped outside the walls, wanting to be allowed in so that the soul and the man could become one, heal, and finally live.

DARK NIGHT OF THE SOUL

The dark night of the soul is a journey into light, a journey
from your darkness into the strength and hidden resources of your soul.
~ Caroline Myss

The pain is unexpected and more powerful than anything I have experienced—indescribable. I don't think I've ever felt such an intense feeling of loss and an inability to escape from the pain. I feel perpetually stuck. The grief after my father's death, the hurt of past lovers, nothing weighed as heavily on me as this. I feel unhinged. The unbearable disquiet in my emotions is foreign; in my normal state, I am calm and can easily regain my balance. I am usually composed, collected, and I can readily bounce back from negative emotions. The ache is so deep, intense, so damn shocking and uncontrollable. I cry a lot. I am confused; I don't know where this intensity is coming from. Is it because the feeling of connectedness is so incredibly deep? This...this is awful. I can't imagine life without him. I love him. This is so different from any love in my life. This is shocking to me, this end and the subsequent pain.

The day after our virtual, but very real, breakup is difficult. No messages from him, waking up knowing he is gone from my life. I can hardly move; I feel depressed and hollow. I am angry at myself for feeling this way. I am a strong woman, independent, confident, and usually in control of my emotions. I would never let them get the better of me. There is nothing that can keep me down. But now I am out of control, completely and irrationally out of balance simply because a man doesn't want me. *This is finished, it's done, move on!* I scream at myself in my head. *I am an adult, mature, confident woman! How the fuck is this happening to me?*

I sob uncontrollably that night, feeling the deep despair. I'm scared; I can't calm down. My inner dialogue is a constant stream of irrational contradictions. I feel stuck. I pace around my house from room to room. It's too much. I fall to my knees, my face on the cold floor, and beg for help. I plead, to God, a higher power, the universe, anything or anyone that can hear me. *Somebody please listen.*

"Please, make me normal again. Fix me, fix my pain. I can't take this, and I don't want it anymore," I plead.

I've never done this before. Except for wishing, I have never prayed with such emotional intensity.

I'm still sobbing on the floor, when a wave of serenity flows through me. I am lighter and the dark shadow is dissipating. Yes, I still feel pain, but I am calm. I am in control. With each released breath, I am more at peace. *What just happened?* Why do I feel better? I hear the words in my head: *Your prayers were answered.* Those are not my words. That is not my voice. I'm a pro at talking to myself, but those are not my words. I feel chills run down my arms and out of the corner of my eye, I see movement. I look up at a silhouette, a figure of a man.

Startled, I scream. The figure disappears. *I shouldn't have screamed!*

"Come back!" I plead.

Silence. *I wonder what this means?* Who or what was that figure? I can't explain this, but I have an inner knowing, a sense, that something, someone, reached out to offer me assistance. I don't question this knowing—I believe it is absolutely true, despite the improbability. This moment becomes the turning point for me, as I move from a dark night to a mysterious phase of what I would eventually learn was an awakening.

The days pass and I am almost myself again. I feel nearly balanced emotionally and mentally. The stability brings with it a logical desire to fix the situation. I am a fixer by nature and always want to find solutions to problems. I believe I can fix anything.

I reflect on my past words and actions. *Did I say anything wrong?* I obsessively read and reread our last text chat, dissecting and analyzing it. *Should I have said something more (or something less)?* Over and over I read the damn exchange. I should delete it, but I don't. The right thing to do is to leave him alone, but that is also the hardest thing to do. I want to reach out to him, swoop in, and fix everything. Take control. Realistically, I know there is nothing I can do. I must simply let him go.

Letting go is more difficult than I expected. I still feel the connection to him. I close my eyes and I can feel the joy, the love, like electricity passing through me. *I want that.* This propels me toward an obsessive desire to find answers. I need to know why. There has to be some deeper meaning to this connection. What I am experiencing is not normal; there must be some explanation for this sense of knowing that we were meant to be together. Plus, I'm still confused about my mystical experience a few days ago. I'm convinced it's directly tied to him. A voice inside me keeps telling me to simply *believe.*

Am I going crazy? Do I need psychological help? Feeling things, hearing things. Even seeing things. Is this just a tough breakup causing mental instability? I receive a crystal-clear answer—no. I know it's not just my usual inner dialogue. This is different. And I trust it. *If I'm not crazy, what is this?* I need to find out more. Maybe it's something related to my connection with him. *We are soulmates? What is a soulmate?* I believe in soulmates, and we have a deep connection. Maybe that's why the emotions and attachment are so deep and the pain so great. We have a special link. I need to fix this. I need answers. I need to fix me. Get back to "normal," like I was before I met him.

What better way to get information than the Internet? I'm off. I search "soulmates." Too much information. I read a few things about soulmates. *Yes, I already know this.* I scroll down. "Twin flames"? I have no idea what the term means, never having seen it, but I'm curious. I click the link. As I quickly read the text, it appears to be a precise description of our relationship. Twin flames are actually one soul, which was split in two. *Why is the soul split in two?* Each half seeks out other in each lifetime so they can unite as one. The physical being has no memory of this, nor any knowledge of the connection at a soul level. Apparently, you can (or do?) meet your twin in every lifetime.

When you first meet, there is a sudden connection, a strong feeling like you have known this person your entire life. It is intense and deep. Sometimes the intensity of these emotions can cause one twin to run away from the other; the feelings are overwhelming. Not only are these fears triggered by the other person, they are also triggered by our own fears. We are basically looking in a mirror when we look at the other twin and we clearly see our shadow side, perhaps things we have been trying to hide, emotions and events that are too difficult to deal with. While one person runs, the other feels abandoned and feels such despair at the loss, they are forced through a "dark night of the soul" and eventually an awakening.

This is it. We are twin flames. This describes everything I have been going through. I feel like I was (probably still am) in a "dark night of the soul." And my answered prayers, the shadow, and sudden belief in many things... Am I awakened? But what am I awakening to?

Oh, there is a solution... On the Internet, there are many solutions, depending on who you want to listen to: prayer, meditation, connecting with your twin via telepathy, and most importantly, healing yourself. The two cannot be one unless both have grown and healed to a certain point of balance and enlightenment. *I believe this.* I really, honestly believe in this, even though it goes against all logical reason. *Am I just grasping at straws? Trying to find hope where there is none? Do I want this to work out so badly that I'm trying to find a way to take control? Could this all be true?* This is so out there, so esoteric, and sounds completely crazy—not at all in line with rational thought. Metaphysical. Spiritual. Divine. I find it very hard to believe in something I cannot see. But yet, I believe this.

I continue reading and it all seems to make sense. However, who the heck would believe any of this if I told them? I decide to keep everything to myself. This is not something you share with just anyone.

But of course, there is a catch: Just because you meet your twin in your lifetime does not mean you will end up with them physically in your lifetime. It may be another future life. You don't know. In fact, it sounds like we have no say over what happens. The universe already has a plan in mind, has already decided before birth if you will unite. Everything comes together in divine timing.

Shit. No control. I cannot control anything, except myself and my own healing. There's no easy solution, no action I can take in the physical world that guarantees we will be together. I need blind faith. That's what this is. Crazy, blind faith. I have so very little faith right now, even though I am slowly awakening my spiritual side.

Believing this requires a leap of faith. As I thought this, suddenly I had a deep intuitive *knowing* that this connection was something beyond the physical. There is something mystical and spiritual that I don't understand yet. I think to myself, *He is your twin flame and there is nothing you can do about it.* I'm hopeful and scared at the same time. The universe and the divine control our union. Wow. I cannot do anything. I cannot fix anything. I cannot control anything. But I'm not satisfied with that answer and I dive deep into the Internet to find an answer to my new question: How do I get him to return?

VII
THE PATH FORWARD

LOOKING
FOR ANSWERS

The days pass slowly, and I have still not heard from him—no text, no call. Although I didn't expect him to reach out, I had hoped he would. I'm OK though, because I am obsessively immersed in finding answers. I've been on the computer for countless hours, reading every single thing I can find about twin flames. There are tons of contradictions, of course—it's only a theory (and a crazy one at that). This is the Internet, where you should only believe half of what you read. Tons of theories, so many opinions. I'm not sure what to believe anymore and, most importantly—what are my next steps? I need to find a way for us to unite. *Don't chase after him.* OK, wasn't planning on that anyway, even though I really wanted to. None of this is fact. All just theory. But I need answers *now*.

The emotions of the twin flame meeting are so intense, and the people are usually not ready for it. Not ready? I felt very ready. *The overwhelming emotions create panic and fear and can cause one of the twins to run away.* Yes, I know that. That's him. *Usually the fear is much deeper than we see at the surface. It is a deep primal fear and, very commonly, fear of abandonment, rejection, or failure, coupled with a lack of self-*

love. The overwhelming emotions are too intense, and the first instinct is to run as fast as they can in the other direction and not look back. It's all starting to make sense. This must be the problem. He is scared of the intense emotions. And the walls— the walls just make it worse! He loves me, but he is afraid to be with me... I believe this with my whole heart.

The other person, the chaser (definitely me), *is left in disbelief, feeling like their heart has been ripped from their chest, an immense pain, which triggers their own fear of abandonment.* And rightly so: I have been abandoned. *It is an undiluted, primal grief, as if an essential part of you has been torn away.* This is how I feel. I have tried to control the pain, tried everything that had usually worked for me, without resolution. I even tried swallowing my sorrow, which literally involves swallowing several times and saying the words in my head, "I'm swallowing my sorrow; it's going away." This has always worked for me, but now all it does is make me feel like I'm going to choke.

However, I find hope. We are twin flames and now that I understand how it all works, I will find a solution and resolve the problem. Patience is important. I need patience, because he will eventually come back. I'm not very patient in general. How long? Some waited years. Shit. I am not waiting years! No way. Nobody is worth years of waiting. *Don't chase him—that will only prolong the running. Let him go.* That's what I'm doing. *But I am not waiting years!* I'm so impatient. Life is too short. I can't wait years. I need to move on. But what if I move on and I'm not supposed to? What if I'm supposed to wait? How will he know that we are twin flames? My head is spinning, and I can't make a decision.

I could try to speed up the process though. One site claims that you can connect with your twin telepathically. Or at least with his higher self. *What is a higher self?* More questions. Meditation can help you relax, clear your mind, and balance your emotions— maybe it can help you connect with someone telepathically. I'm going off the deep end. This is not science. Am I so desperate that I would believe something that is way out there? I don't feel crazy right now though. I feel positively sane and now I can actually take action.

Meditation. I'm doing it. I sit down and close my eyes. But my thoughts won't stop, and after five minutes, I'm bored. Music helps a little, but I still don't feel like I'm meditating. What does it mean anyway? Peace? Nirvana? What is nirvana? More questions for Google. I stumble upon guided meditations on YouTube. This is perfect! There are so many of them and I try several and, slowly over the next few days, I finally stop the thoughts from filling my head with cluttered noise.

Over the next week, I spend some time meditating. I also start writing, keeping a journal of my thoughts and emotions, something I hadn't done in a long time. The journal is first filled with hopelessness and confusion. *I really love him and want him to come back.* The words make me cringe. I sound immature. I question the *why* behind my feelings, the sense of desperation. It's not healthy. There is just such a powerful connection between us, I can't imagine losing that feeling forever. I still cry a lot, especially when I write. All the emotions come pouring out when I write. I'm not sure it's making me feel better, but at least I'm getting a better understanding of myself. I write pages, this journal becomes habit—I can't live a day without self-evaluation and introspection.

I continue with my everyday life. My birthday comes and goes. I spend a lot of time with my family, friends, and fill my days with many distractions. I'm moving on, I tell myself. *He didn't remember my birthday.* But how would he know when it was? *I think I told him.* Did he even know? I chastise myself for even imagining that he should've wished me happy birthday. He is still running, nowhere to be seen. The week was full of good, despite the lingering sadness. I'm still obsessed with learning more about twins, but I also decide that I will be OK. I'm fine if I never hear from him again. I'm strong and independent, I tell myself, and nothing can keep me down for very long.

A PICTURE-PERFECT PAST

Despite my adamant proclamations to myself about moving on, my curiosity and desire to know *everything* permeates my daily thoughts. I decide I need to know when (there is no *if* in my mind) he will return, and we will be together. Not knowing the answers and being faced with too much uncertainty is not acceptable. Being in control of situations (and my emotions) and using my intuition to guide me is the only way I can make decisions. But get this—since he left, my strong sense of knowing what to do is gone. I'm totally confused and frozen with indecision; the feeling in my gut that often tells me *yes* or *no* is murky.

How can I get clear answers? I need help clearing the clutter and finding the truth. So I spontaneously decide to get a psychic reading. I have never done this before. Getting a reading always sounded amusing, and I was curious. While there are some that claim they can read the future, I'm a rational person. The future is not set in stone—the future is ours to change. It's unlikely that I will find answers. Probably just further evidence of my temporary insanity. I decide I have nothing to lose.

The reading was, well...a strange experience. I didn't ask her anything except what I wanted to know—what is going on with him and why we have such a deep connection. I am very skeptical that this is going to work, but I feel I have no other solution.

I'm surprised when she guesses his initials. She also describes the overall situation exactly. But what really shocks me is when she suddenly stops the reading. She says she can't go any further—there is a locked door, something is blocking her from finishing the reading. A wall, she says, a wall surrounds the door. His wall. *It's so strong, even a psychic can't get through,* I tell myself. She also explains that the locked door is related to me. She says I need healing, particularly in my throat chakra. I have no idea what a chakra is, but she explains that it relates to communication and the ability to understand and speak your inner truth "purely."

This makes sense. I've always had a problem speaking my mind, letting things out, speaking from my heart, releasing emotions. Words are trapped, and I feel, also, my sorrow. Maybe after all of these years of swallowing my sorrow, everything is clogged. She describes a negative energy that needs to be cleaned out, something I have carried from childhood. She says there's something in my possession that has to be destroyed. Emotions? No, a physical item, she replies.

I only partially believe this. *Is she just making things up?* I have very few items from my childhood except some special baby outfits and some pictures. And how can destroying an item clear the energy? This sounds crazy, like witchcraft. Yes, I'm willing to believe in many things, but destroying something to release some sort of—curse? I'm skeptical. This is a waste of time.

She returns part of my money and again tells me what I need to do—find the object and destroy it, heal my chakras, and then she would continue the reading. She says I can set up a chakra healing session with her, but I don't trust her, so I tell her I will be in touch.

I am perplexed. *She is wrong.* She was right about a few things, but it was probably just luck or coincidence. At home, I try to think of what childhood possessions she might be talking about, but I can't think of anything but the pictures...the pictures... that's it. I'm filled with an illuminating, intuitive feeling about the pictures. I actually see a particular picture in my mind. *Look at the baby album.* I hear those words in my head.

I run upstairs and immediately turn to the back of the front cover of the album, where there is a small compartment behind the photo. I gently peel back the disintegrating Scotch tape. Inside are two handwritten notes. I should be shocked—I had no idea they were there, but instead I'm only mildly surprised. *I somehow knew they were always there.* Another inexplicable intuitive feeling. I open each one carefully; they are old and look like they will crumble apart. The notes are both from my biological father. The notes don't say anything significant, and are in fact, very ordinary. I don't feel moved—I don't feel anything. They are neutral. The notes both say the same thing: "this note is a gift to you." I call my mother and ask her about the notes. She is more surprised than I am. She is the one who organized the album and it was in her possession until she gave it to me a few years ago. She has no idea how the notes got there.

At this point, I realize that I need to destroy the notes. The psychic's premonition and the notes' mysterious appearance are enough proof. I feel suddenly fearful. I decide it doesn't matter. They have to be destroyed.

I burn them. As they burn, I feel relief. When they are nothing but ashes, I feel closure. Such a strange feeling, but something that should have been done a long time ago is now complete. I then take the ashes to one of my favorite spots along the river and scatter them in the water. *Goodbye, dark energy. Or whatever you are.* I feel as if a tremendous burden has been lifted. I'm stunned by my feelings. It was such a simple action. I wish had known about the notes a long time ago.

I'm surprised that I thought of looking in my baby album. I never would have thought there was anything in there! Is there really some force at work, helping me regain my balance? Or do I have some sort of ability to see things? Am I psychic? Is this just a coincidence? A small voice in my head says *no.* A voice. I am crazy! But I don't feel crazy. Then of course, all crazy people believe they are not crazy. If I think I am crazy, does that make me sane? I go back and forth, logically trying to sort through this.

I take a deep breath. I decide that I will believe that something magical is happening. I will believe the psychic, I will believe that my burning of the notes brought me relief, even if I don't logically understand why or where this is all going. I decide to have faith. Crazy or not, does not matter at this point. Many people with crazy ideas and mystical beliefs have often been proven right. I will be open and go with the flow...

EXPECT THE UNEXPECTED

Yes, I sometimes talk to my stepfather and often ask him for guidance. This is probably one of the few spiritual actions I readily accepted as "normal" before all of these strange events started to happen. He always gave valuable advice when he was alive. I often go to his tree, where his ashes are buried, and just try to feel his presence. I'm not sure I ever received any answer or felt his presence, but it comforts me to think that he can hear me. I visit his tree out on the farm. I try to sense if he is here with me now. Can I ask him for help? I don't feel anything. I have no idea if he is really here with me. *I wish he were.*

Later, I'm home and getting ready for bed. I walk past my kitchen, and for the second time, I see a shadow of a man standing by the sink. It startles me and I scream. The figure vanishes. *I have to stop screaming. Maybe he has something to tell me and if I keep screaming, I will never know what he has to say.* I stand there for a moment, waiting for his return. Nothing.

Although after the fact I sensed the presence was peaceful and benevolent, I really don't want to start seeing ghosts. Being haunted does not sound enjoyable. Was this just another affirmation of my potential insanity? Or was the presence really there? I wanted to believe in something, but I was also terrified at the thought of these things actually existing. Was it my stepfather? Was he responding to my "prayer" at the tree? Yes. I firmly believe it was him and he was letting me know he is here for me.

I crawl into bed to write in my journal. I finish writing, put my journal away, and spontaneously decide to pray. Pray to my stepfather and really anyone or anything that will hear me. I don't know what is out there, but it can't hurt to pray, right? I'm not completely in though—I pray half-heartedly. *What difference will it make?* I ask for guidance: Is he my twin flame? Do I wait for him? Do I move on? *Please tell me what's going on!* I need more information. I get little comfort from praying, which to me seems like I'm talking to myself and further proof of my emotional imbalance. But it becomes a ritual, integrated with my daily meditation. My search for answers.

I do in fact feel more balanced and emotionally stable since I started this "inner work." I ask—what should I do about him? *Wait.* I keep hearing the answer—wait. Wait for what? Does this mean we will be together one day? *What am I waiting for? Him?* I deeply sense and believe that he will reach out to me soon. Just a feeling. My intuition. *Tomorrow* comes another response. Tomorrow? Tomorrow as in tomorrow or in weeks, days, years? Is tomorrow another dimension? Another lifetime? I fall asleep.

Buzzz. My phone vibrates. I have a text message. It's five a.m. *Who the hell is texting me at five a.m.?* I look at my phone. It's him, out of the blue. I'm surprised. Shocked. I remember what I heard last night: *tomorrow.* After some short, bizarrely casual chit chat—*is he ignoring the fact that he walked away?*—he asks if he can come over that night to talk. Without hesitation, I say yes. I'm ecstatic that he texted me...but still, I'm confused. I wasn't expecting this so soon, but I will hear what he has to say.

The moment he walks in, I feel the connection. No walls. I try not to get pulled in, but I have really missed him, and I let my guard down. We exchange pleasantries and I offer him a drink. We sit on opposite ends of the couch.

"So, what do you want to talk about?" I ask casually.

"Well," he pauses, "I've been thinking that I'd like to continue seeing you and see if we can work things out."

He stands up, starts pacing as he continues.

"You know, these walls... I really don't want them to be in the way. I am open right now; they aren't here. I want them to stay down. What I feel for you..." he stops.

There are tears in his eyes. He does love me. I sensed it before, but now it's undeniable.

"I'm scared," he says. "It's so intense, it's too much."

I'm trying to find the right thing to say. I stay silent and listen.

He sits down next to me and says, "I'd like to slow things down. This all happened too fast."

"What are you afraid of?" I ask.

I start to cry—I can't help it; his pain is my pain and I can feel his emotions. He hugs me and now he's crying too. *Oh, I missed this.* Not the crying. The physical connection. We kiss and I'm gone. I'm all in again and my fears about the relationship evaporate. *I can take things slowly.*

Of course, we sleep together and, of course, he stays the night. Not quite the definition of slowing things down. I'm comforted that he completely opened his heart to me, shared his feelings, the pain, his desire to tear down the walls (goddamn walls). I feel very optimistic that everything's going to work out.

My optimism doesn't last long. As soon as I wake up and roll over and touch him, I sense the distance. He hasn't even opened his eyes—he is sound asleep—and I feel he is leaving again. So quickly, he was all in and now he is sneaking away. *Stop. You are projecting your fears.* However, he opens his eyes and I see it clearly. He isn't just running, he is, in fact, nearly gone. I don't say a word. I know now when he is closed like that, nothing I say will make any difference.

After he leaves and the day progresses, the feelings of sadness and loss return. *He is gone.* Again. Disconnected. Overcoming my fears, I call him. We talk for over an hour. Again, a very meaningful and honest conversation. We both agree we want to be together, but the situation is too complicated and difficult. I don't know what to do. He doesn't know what to do. He suggests no sex. The sex is just too good, too intense, he says. I'm confused. Role reversal. He explains that the intensity of the emotions he feels with me during sex are too overwhelming. Although I am initially surprised by this, I also have a deep understanding of what he means. I felt the intensity, although, to me, the intensity was a positive experience. Again, this proves to me that I am not imagining the deep connection we share, that there is something mystical and intense between us. So we decide there will be no sex and that we will take things at a slower pace. I will miss the sex, but I decide to go with the flow of this new plan.

I almost want to tell him about my twin flame discovery. It explains a lot about the uncomfortable intensity of his emotions. I decide against it. I'm sure it would either freak him out or he would think I'm completely insane. I'm confident that this will work out, and I am ready for us to move forward together.

I am back in my blissful state. We have some wonderful connected moments over the next week. Deep conversations, constantly finishing each other's sentences, enjoying each other's company. This is when I start noticing strange coincidences. The same words come up several times in one day, with different people. Electric. Unexpectedly I see and hear that word everywhere— in news articles, conversations, random writing on the sides of trucks. And Africa. Together, we experience allusions to Africa. Random phrases become not so random. I've never heard the acronym YOLO (you only live once), although it is a mantra I strive to live by, and then I hear it three times in the same day—in something I read, in a conversation with my kids, and in a conversation with him.

The coincidences continue. He and I speak the same words simultaneously, or realize we are thinking the same thoughts. I think about him, and lo and behold, within seconds he texts me. This happens countless times. I take notice and document everything, not understanding what any of it means, but eventually realizing that these curious occurrences are not mere coincidences, but synchronicities. The synchronicities confirm that I—we—are on the right path.

This time the distance comes slower, but it comes, nevertheless. I am fearful. I try to remain calm. I can't and don't want to believe he is leaving again. I wake up feeling anxious and unbalanced. The sense of disconnectedness is the same feeling as before; he is distancing himself and I will be abandoned again.

When he texts me later, I can actually sense the distance in the texts, although he doesn't really say anything that indicates he is walling himself up. It's just a feeling. It's as if I can feel the truth behind the words, despite the neutrality of the words. *What is going on?* Everything seemed to be flowing so well recently. I am open again, fearless, and ready to let myself be vulnerable with him. I do think part of me knew it was inevitable, but I hoped it wouldn't have been so soon. And especially when things were so effortless, balanced, and *perfect*. I realize people cannot change overnight. I was ready and not ready for what would come. It is too hard now to go with the flow, but I decide not to think too much about it and live my life. Block it out and ignore it, for now.

THE GUIDING LIGHT

'm not very successful at blocking out my fear that he will leave again. I try to block out the negative feelings that arise from his growing distance. *Ignore it.* I can't. I decide not to say anything to him since I'm not completely sure about the validity of my feelings. I try to go with the flow and rationalize that perhaps these feelings are simply my own fears of abandonment. I feel off balance. I am emotionally up and down. I know I need to heal my chakras, but I'm not sure what that means.

I return to my computer, my faithful—and only—source of information. I learn about the chakras and how to balance them with energy. Reiki, a term I had heard before but knew nothing about. *How do I do this?* I recall there is someone I know that does this type of healing. I send her an email and ask for her advice.

I don't hear back from her right away but am surprised to run into her at an friend's luncheon. Whether by coincidence or synchronicity, the woman I reached out to was invited by one of my friends to the lunch. Another chance encounter? I believe it is not chance. I speak with her, nervously, because I have no idea what energy healing actually is, and we schedule a time for me to come into her office.

I'm anxious and unsure of what to expect. Could this actually work? Clear my chakras? She explains the process and we talk a bit about what I am going through. I find myself confiding in her about him, and the situation. I feel like I'm in therapy. I feel relief because I have not told anyone many of the details of my relationship with him and the strange things that have been happening to me.

I slowly ease into the session, breathing deeply, trying to remain calm while my insane mind runs in a million different directions. I'm thinking about everything that is going on in my life. Thinking about him. Thinking about what I would make for dinner, wondering if this would work. I grow calmer when she finally lays her hands on me, starting on my head. I relax. My mind decluttered, I finally find peace.

As she moves over different parts my body, her hands gently touching each chakra, I feel her power. I feel warmth, a soft, electric buzz. I hear a buzzing vibration in my ears. As she works, I start to feel incredibly sad, and I grow scared. *Was this making things worse?* However, she releases a huge sigh, and I immediately sigh deeply in response. I feel a release of those negative emotions. With that breath, I liberate my pain. Incredible.

The most astonishing aspect of the session are the vivid visual images that I experience. I feel like I'm dreaming, but I'm wide awake. I see green moving lights, a spider web of lights, then orange and yellow. It is incredibly peaceful. I want to stay in the beautiful light. *She is helping me.* To my surprise, I also see objects, things...visions? Similar to my meditations, but clearer, more defined. I see a shark and a woman. The woman is not scared of the shark. I have no idea what this means, but I resolve to remember it.

I walk out of her office a new person. *Yet another thing to believe in*, I tell myself. I'm driving home, letting cars ease in front of me, smiling at all the aggressive drivers, taking my time, when I feel momentarily dizzy and see a picture. That is the only way I can describe it. A clear and very real picture of a wedding. My wedding. With him, on my island, on a beach. We are standing, and the wind is blowing my hair. I'm wearing a short, white, strapless dress and he is wearing a white shirt and khakis. I know immediately this is a vision of the future. And it will happen. I can't explain how I know this. I just know. I smile and I believe.

I remain peaceful and balanced, and these feelings stay with me for many days, despite the fact that I still sense he is distancing himself. My vision has given me hope.

That night I dream about a hawk. The hawk is perched on the steeple of a church, looking straight at me. He opens his wings, flies over me, and into a forest. I wake, feeling like the hawk was trying to tell me something. I look up the symbolism of the hawk. *The hawk is a messenger of the spirit world*, I read. *It symbolizes the ability to use intuition and higher vision. The universe wants you to expand your knowledge and your wisdom.* Perfect; that's what I am trying to do. *Yes!* I want to learn everything. I feel powerful and, most importantly, I am at peace.

Unfortunately, the feeling doesn't last. The next time I see him, we go to the movies. I sit next to him in the theater, and the distance is unmistakable. He's not even present, like the man I know is gone and a stranger has taken his place. We hold hands a few times, but it's very awkward. Cold. I feel uncomfortable. Unsure of everything. Again, confusion and disarray. I am not expecting this after the positive energy I felt a few days ago. Yes, I knew there would likely be challenging moments, but nothing like this complete withdrawal.

I don't hear from him all weekend. I don't expect to hear from him, since he has his son all weekend. But still. If someone wants you, they will at least make an effort to connect. When I finally hear from him, we plan to have dinner a few days later. However, the night before, as I'm getting into bed, I know he will cancel. I'm not surprised when he texts me the next morning and says he can't make it. This confirms that my intuition, my predictive sense, is spot on. I can sense things before they happen. I feel like I can predict the future.

My mind gets the best of me. I wonder: did my fear of him cancelling cause him to cancel—the Law of Attraction? Or did I truly predict the future? I've been reading about the Law of Attraction, and it scares me that my thoughts can have a direct effect on events. If you think positively, you will get positive results. But if you think negative thoughts, well, then prepare yourself for a negative outcome. I've been trying to remain positive, thinking this will make a difference. However, the negative thoughts creep in—I can't help it—and I feel like I can't control the creation of my reality. Who knew the spiritual world was so complicated and could cause so much angst?

I am very upset by his cancellation. Yes, he has a good reason, kid-related, but I also sense he is relieved to have an excuse. I wish he could be a bit more disappointed that we couldn't spend time together. Again, this all happens via text. I sense there is a deeper meaning behind the words he types.

My balance is gone. I fall apart. Again. Instead of just accepting that, yes, he does love me but is scared shitless, and taking a mature approach, I turn the whole situation into a huge pity party and wallow in despair. I can't understand how his walls, his fear, could overpower the beautiful power of love. Therefore, it must not be love. I realize that I am more angry than sad this time. This is new. Not only am I angry at him, but I am also angry at myself, for continually being pulled back into the energy of blind faith. *Idiot.* I say nothing to him about my disappointment. I act like I don't care. I need to focus on regaining my balance.

I realize that regardless of whether he is my twin flame or not, I need to let him go. He can't give me what I want and need right now, and it is far too painful for me. I know my value and my worth and I do not need a man to prove that, especially one who is incapable of expressing his love. I am a giver. I gave everything to him and while he sometimes reciprocated, most of the time he didn't. I will not continue like this. Ending this is the right thing to do.

HEAL THYSELF

practice self-healing, or solo-Reiki as I call it. I'm learning to harness my own energy, directing energy to each of the chakras, trying to find my way to the images of light I saw at my first Reiki session. I have no idea what I'm doing, but I'm positive it will work. It's a struggle at first, and it takes me forty-five minutes to achieve the same level of relaxation that I experienced at my first session. Finally, I see the green, webbed light. *Can I heal myself?* I thought. *Can I be a healer?* I keep my hands on my abdomen, the solar plexus and sacral chakras, and for several minutes see the colorful, flashing lights. I am peaceful. *I can do this!*

I'm so enthusiastic, I practice several times during the day. The next few times, it is much easier to reach the green webbing. I imagine the green webbing as a place, a state of being—nirvana. Wherever or whatever it is, it's powerful. My mind is clear and I am taking in the positive energy when I see a vision of a naked woman in front of a golden yurt. She has just given birth to a child and she is holding her placenta. Is she me? *Please don't eat the placenta,* I tell her. *I have given birth to something.* My healing? *What have I given birth to?* Faith. I feel the power and significance of this moment. I have given birth to my potential and I need to have faith in the universe and in my own ability to initiate change. I'm not one hundred percent sure what this means yet but, of course, I write it down for later reflection.

Faith. Does this mean faith in myself or faith in the universe? I am scared. Faith. I thought I had faith, but maybe it was simply artificial, phony faith. Am I supposed to have faith that he will rush to me and confess his love, even though everything that is happening in reality goes against the fairy tale ending? Does having faith in something that seems impossible make a difference? Could we be reunited, if only I believed? So many questions. I want to believe in the power of positive thinking. That I can change reality. But I realize I very rarely feel the positivity one hundred percent. I can espouse positive words all day long, but my feelings contradict my language.

I continue with my self-healing, practicing every day—writing, meditating, and reading. This is my new obsession: healing myself. Except this time, my obsession is not centered on fixing the relationship. My goal to become whole and balanced and take care of my own emotional and spiritual health. I know this will lead me forward, whatever my path.

While we hadn't officially broken up, I sensed things were pretty much over. A text here and there from him, but really, nothing earth-shattering. I ask him how he's feeling, and he admits he is hibernating, taking needed time alone. I already know this—it's obvious from the lack of communication, plus I sense it intuitively. I realize it's time to take action.

I finally tell him I can't continue like this anymore. It is too uncertain, with the constant back and forth, and the unpredictability of the distances hurts me. He agrees. Again, this is all via text, disappointing, but somehow this has become our norm. We decide not to see each other. I know he will end things eventually anyway. It's better for me to do it now. Enough is enough.

I wonder though, if I had not ended things, what would have happened? *Would he have kept running and ignored me? Would he have realized his mistake and come running back to me?* It doesn't matter. Preempting him, I could prevent being abandoned. Rejecting him, I could prevent him from rejecting me. This is the best way to end things. Yes, I could have stayed, waited things out, but I sensed it was just a matter of time until it was over anyway. I could have hung on, but I was really unhappy and not getting what I needed. *Did I do the right twin flame thing? Is there a right thing to do?* In my heart, I know I have to let him go. I need to take care of *me*. I need the separation from him, as much as he needs the separation from me. I sense that I hurt him. Or maybe I am just trying to make myself feel better.

I wake up the next morning feeling surprisingly refreshed and positive. I am free all week, my son is at his dad's, so I make a spontaneous decision to take a trip across the river to a quaint little town. Maybe go to an antique shop, have coffee, walk around. I haven't been there in years, but the thought pops into my head and I decide to go. It'll be a good way to clear my head and get him out of my thoughts.

I take the ferry across the river. It's such a beautiful day. Sunny and warm, and I feel peaceful. I feel the calm of the river as the ferry floats across the water. Perfect.

I wander into an antique shop, drawn to the beautiful glass pieces. I'm a sucker for beautiful, colored glass. I find a set of old blue champagne flutes and am about to purchase them, when something tells me to stop. *OK, I won't.* I continue meandering through the cluttered displays, appreciating the history. I go upstairs and walk down a hallway, as if I know exactly where I'm going. I step into a small room full of old books. I leaf through a few, nothing interesting. Suddenly I see a book with my mother's name on it—her very rare, Portuguese name—and I grab it immediately. It's an art book, full of beautiful textile art, quilts, framed three-dimensional paintings. Lovely. I ease the book back into its rightful spot, but I don't push it all the way in, in case I decide to buy it. I then notice another book nearby with his mother's name on it. Strange. I pull out the book. It's a fiction book and not particularly interesting. What is interesting though, are the names of both of our mothers showing up like this, nearly side by side on a bookshelf—what are the chances? This is not a just coincidence, but a synchronicity.

I am about to grab both books and buy them, when I notice the title of the book between them: *Born to Heal.* Healing. *That's what I'm trying to do.* So strange. I quickly skim through the intro and read the back cover. The book is about a man named Bill Gray, who used electro-magnetic energy to heal people of physical ailments. I have never heard of him, but I know intuitively that this is the book I am meant to buy. The books with our mothers' names were there to point me in the right direction, to force me to look at the book between them. It was a sign. There is no doubt in my mind. I bought the book. And of course, the sparkling blue champagne flutes. I couldn't resist.

As I'm checking out, I tell the woman behind the counter my story about finding the book. I tell her how I woke up this morning, knowing I had to take this trip. I ordinarily would not share this information. I already sometimes think I am crazy, so why let other people think it also? *Stop talking*, I tell myself. Unbelievably, she accepts my story as if it's normal.

"I'm surprised you believe me," I say.

"I believe in many things," she answers matter-of-factly. "I have seen and heard some amazing things." She carefully wraps my glasses and continues, "I'm a medium. I pick up messages from the spirit world."

I'm impressed and intrigued. How could she openly talk to people about these things? And how did she learn to be a medium? How does it work? My mind is filled with questions, but she excuses herself to help another customer.

"Oh, here's my card. Let me know if you need any help." She hands me her business card, smiles, and walks away.

I leave with more questions than when I arrived, but I have a book, and maybe reading this book will give me answers. And now I have something else I want to learn about: mediumship. I believe that my reasons for coming on this trip were to find this book and talk to this woman. I took her card but didn't really think I would reach out. Still, I would keep it just in case. I went home in peace, thinking that the pieces to the puzzle were finally coming together. Most importantly, I realized the importance of following my intuition and going with the flow. I need to leave my fate in the hands of a higher power and have absolute trust. Trust in the messages. Trust that whatever path I am guided to is for an important reason and potentially will lead to answers.

I'm driving home, just having crossed over on the ferry, when I start to feel dizzy. *Oh no. Not a migraine.* I pull over, hoping it passes quickly. I close my eyes and wait. Usually I'm OK after a few minutes. Out of nowhere, a vision: this time I see the words, "Everything will be OK." And then, "March." And finally, "Three." I have no idea what this means. Is this about the numbers? Should I play the lottery with the numbers from my dream in March? I have no idea. Another piece is added to my ever-growing puzzle. Something else to solve. The dizziness goes away and I continue home.

As I'm writing in my journal about my experiences, I can't help but try to tie them to our relationship. I don't really see a clear connection, except that someone needs healing. We both do. My intuition has grown; I feel I can easily sense others' feelings, especially his. I can tell when he is distant, when he is open. I feel like I can even see what he's doing at times. Sometimes, I feel pain, and I know it's not my pain. It's his pain. I know it. *We are connected, still,* I think. I wonder if he can sense me? For now, I don't want to sense him anymore. Feeling his pain is almost worse than my own.

CONNECTING
THE PIECES

The days pass, the autumn days grow shorter, and winter approaches.

My journal is filling up quickly. I go back and read my old entries. It bothers me that I was so lost, confused, and in pain. The way I described my emotions, I don't like the way I sound at all. Have I changed that much? I hope so because I sounded like a blithering, lovelorn fool. There are still remnants, but I am a lot more balanced now.

I read my entry about the numbers. I still don't know what they mean. 12, 15, 18, 20, 22, and of course 3. I play on each day of the month that corresponds to a number, Powerball only. I still haven't won. I'm sure that the numbers have a deeper meaning. Plus, I now have a few new numbers to add to the mix. I've been dreaming and seeing several other numbers repeatedly. I even created a cipher solver, each number representing a letter. I came up with the letters LORTVCIHDIAE. Gobbledygook. All of it nonsense. I can form random words here and there, but nothing that makes any sense. I will have to come back to this. Maybe it's not complete yet.

Then it hits me. *What if it's a date?* 12/15/18, is December 15, 2018. Next month. And 20 and 22 military time, is 8:22 p.m. Was something going to happen on that date, at that time? And what about the number 3? What does that mean? How is the date related to anything? I guess I have to wait and see what happens on that date.

Maybe I'm focusing on the wrong thing. The numbers look like they could be a longitude/latitude, so I input them into a map. I land in Africa. Chad. Right in the middle of the desert. I don't see any connection to anything going on, except that he and I both lived in Africa as kids. I research Chad, from an archeological standpoint, and read that scientists found a skull in Chad that could be one of the oldest-known relatives of modern humans. Then I notice that some of my letters, derived from the numbers, spell CHAD. *And? What does that mean?* I'm on a wild goose chase. This doesn't make sense. Why is Chad so important? The beginning of humankind? Consciousness? Maybe Adam and Eve. I have no idea.

After working on these puzzles for several hours, I'm exhausted. I take a break. I will have to come back to this later.

The images during meditation continue to come at me very quickly. I'm sure that even though I write them down immediately after, I probably miss many. A boy in blue footie pajamas, jumping on a bed. A portly, short, one-eyed man, a man with a red beard and an old-fashioned elvish-type hat...a volcano, the Dead Sea. Hawks, churches, and words. I think I can write a book based on just the symbols in my journal! Today, it was stamps. I saw some stamps and heard the message, *find the stamps.* Letters? I look in my memory box. Lots of letters, but nothing out of the ordinary. All the stamps look normal. *Stamps in May...what? A letter in May? Will I receive a letter in May?* I write everything in my journal, not understanding the meaning, and hoping that one day I will learn what they mean.

Throughout this time, I keep busy, but still I long for him. I continue pushing those feelings aside, trying to move forward with my own life and trying to release him completely. *I will not regress,* I tell myself. However, I failed. I did make one tiny (maybe not so tiny), stupid mistake when I was feeling particularly desperate. I texted him. Yes, I was weak.

Me: When you are ready to talk, let me know. I'm happy to get together.

I regretted it the second I sent it. I'm supposed to be leaving him alone to figure things out. But I felt I had so much to say. All my new insights and discoveries—I wanted to share them with him. I was relieved that he didn't reply.

This lapse in judgment propels me to work even harder on healing myself. I write a list in my journal—my fears, my desires, a totally honest assessment of what I feel I need to work on. This forces me to examine negative aspects that I have ignored. My shadow side. Most people are terrified to look at themselves in the mirror and admit the negative aspects of themselves, things that we keep from the rest of the world. But I know it's a necessary step to healing and becoming whole. I am impatient for happiness and fulfillment. Sometimes I feel like happiness should come much quicker than it has, as if offered up on a platter. *Here, here is your happiness, Love, The Universe.* I'm slowly realizing that happiness comes from within. Only I can work to make myself balanced and happy...not someone else, not an outside force. I need to find that happiness within myself, loving even the dark aspects. I will take care of me, heal myself and my complex issues. There are many, and they run deep. I try to let go of my expectations and just *be.* I let the feelings pass through me, without judgment and with complete acceptance.

I have worked so hard on myself. I believe healing will take me on the path toward freedom. Freedom from fear, from longing for what I can't have, freedom to be authentic. Most of the time, I'm balanced, content, and have very good days. Things seem to be falling into place. Then, out of the blue, I feel a stabbing physical pain in my abdomen that grows into emotional pain. It's so sudden and without cause, it frustrates me. *This is not my pain. How can I be feeling someone else's emotions?* They are his emotions, I am convinced. His confusion, his anger, his pain that he refuses to release. I cry for no reason. These are not my tears. They feel foreign, separated from me. Is it possible? I can't explain many things that are happening anyway, so I simply accept them, let them flow. I need to keep myself relatively sane and hope for clarity later.

The anniversary of my stepfather's death hits me much harder this year. I think about the phone call from my sister in the middle of the night. How I knew as soon as I answered the phone that he was gone. She said, *come* and I knew. She said it again, *come.*

I told her: I'm *coming right now.* It's funny how some moments stay etched in your mind. A difficult day. A loss of hope, a loss of stability. I remember thinking: *Who will I go to for advice? Who will hold the family together?* It was he who saved us, entering our lives as a solid, practical, yet loving and patient man, dropping his anchor in a safe harbor, saving us from the chaos of the stormy lives. I felt lost without him, like our whole family would now fall apart because he was the one that kept us all safe. His advice was invaluable. I would listen, learn, and sometimes still did my own thing anyway. But I always listened and appreciated his words. He was practical, while I was a wild and impulsive decision maker at times. Tempered with his words, my decisions felt sound. Losing him was like losing my balance. I feel like I am all instinct now, trying to use only my intuition and making critical decisions by myself. *Somehow this is good for me,* I thought.

My thoughts of him and his practicality make me want my life back, my old self, confident, emotionally stable. I want my family back. After his death, our family felt like it was fractured. Arguments, distance, everyone in emotional upheaval. But I realized that these things were necessary. We are healing. Now I just need to find my own path. It will come. I know he is with me, watching over me and protecting me from danger, so I continue to talk to him whenever I need his guidance. Who knows? Many of these crazy things are probably messages from him, but they are so confusing and I can't understand them. *What do I do? I can't understand the messages.* I am paralyzed, fearing that not understanding will take me down the wrong path. I want to make decisions from a place of love, not fear. *How can I tell the difference?* How do I go back to who I was? This new me, unstable, confused, and lonely, wants perfect me back.

I need more help. I'm impatient. I need to know the future; I need to understand why this is happening and if I am on the right path. Is he, my soulmate, coming back? I start to doubt that he loves me, that I just created that story for comfort. I run into a woman who reads auras. She can even use photos, so I ask her for a reading. She reads two pictures, mine and his.

She tells me, "This relationship will never work. Not now, not in the future."

"Why?" I ask. I'm quite concerned.

"Darkness. I see dark, unresolved issues in him that may never be sorted out. While he appreciates your light, he does not love you. He is draining your energy; he wants it for himself because it makes him feel lighter, happier, but at the same time he is fearful that you will sense his darkness."

What? I'm dumbstruck. I don't want to believe her, but she seems authentic. She has many great reviews and I'm supposed to believe in *everything* now. Was he really sucking out my positive energy and filling me with toxic sludge? I need to let him go. He needs to find his own way out of darkness and into the light. I want no part of this!

On the other hand, what makes her right and my intuition wrong? I don't know what to believe anymore. How can she be right? This would make me wrong about everything. Have I been wasting my time on something that has no possibility of ever happening? I'm even more confused after this reading. I think I'd better just move on, no matter what I feel.

I am moving on. Decision made. Surprisingly, I don't feel sadness, but relief. This makes it much easier to let go, knowing that there is something wrong with him—or at least possibly wrong. However, I contradict myself again. Letting go makes me feel like I'm giving up. I feel that my spiritual awakening is because of him, and all the new discoveries I've made are tied to him. Thus, aren't we supposed to be together, happily ever after?

The reality is, his problems seem too complex and deep. Too insurmountable. I turn my attention inward, accepting that his problems are not my concern. I have to focus on my own growth and learning. I feel my heart and intuition pulling me in his direction, but the emotional and spiritual chaos I am going through is causing me too much confusion. There is nothing I can do except move on, walk away. Let go of the fantasies I have created. I finally delete our text conversation, a long collection of exchanges that started right after we met. A very big step for me. I promise myself I will focus on myself. No more reliving the past. I am free.

THE RED ROSE

I n my quest for spiritual knowledge, I sign up for a mediumship
workshop. Why not learn how to communicate with the dead?
Since I might be crazy anyway, I have nothing to lose. Although
I believe people can communicate with those who have passed on,
I'm not sure I believe that I can actually do it. I'm curious and
it's a fun distraction. Plus, I may meet some like-minded spiritual
people to share my thoughts with.

Before the class, I decide to have a personal session with the
instructor. I'm curious and maybe I will find some answers.

I expected a stereotypical fortune teller, from the old carnival
days. She is normal. She acts and looks like someone I would
see in daily life. I wanted her to be mystical and mysterious—
somehow, I think that would add some authenticity to the reading.
Go with the flow.

I'm a bit nervous and start to have second thoughts, but her
soothing personality calms me down. She asks me to close my
eyes and relax and to breathe deeply. I can do this; it's just like
meditation. She says a protective blessing to shield us from dark
spirits. OK, I'm a little anxious. Go *away, dark spirits*. I try to relax.

She asks my ancestors, my deceased loved ones, to please
come forward and deliver any messages.

After a few minutes, she says, "There is someone here, an older man. Tall, with short, gray hair. I feel a lot of love coming from him. He used to take you to the park when you were little."

I'm surprised at her accuracy.

"That's my grandfather," I reply.

"He says he is watching over you and your family." The medium is smiling.

"Wait, someone else wants to come in, and he is very impatient. He is a shorter man, bald, very lively. He is dancing!"

I have no idea who this is. Dancing bald man? The only dancing bald man I remember is from one of my meditations.

"He teases your grandfather and they laugh. They are both playfully fighting for your attention."

"Ah, I know who it is. It's his brother-in-law, my great-uncle. They used to argue about who would take me to the park," I reply.

I'm amazed that these two people appeared. But I want to talk to my father.

"Is my father there?" I ask.

She pauses and says, "Someone else popped in, a woman with short, gray hair, very petite."

I don't recognize the woman, although I would realize later that she is my aunt.

"Wait. She is gone. Let's see who is coming next." She pauses.

"I'm getting something else, but I'm not exactly sure where it's coming from. Somebody...they want you to know that your spirit guides have been sending you messages. Sometimes these are symbols, numbers. Visions. They know you don't understand everything yet, but you will in time. Be patient."

Of course, all of these visions and dreams and nonsensical symbols. Now it all makes sense. It's not my imagination. But I really want to understand the meaning now—these messages feel very important.

I really need to know.

I ask her, "Can they tell me what everything means and why this is all happening to me? I'm so confused about so many things..."

She interrupts, "Wait, someone is here. He is tall, very handsome. He is older, but his hair is brown. He is a very admired man; he helped many people in his life. He has an accent, British?" She smiles knowingly.

"It's my father. He's South African," I whisper. I feel happiness and sadness all at once. "Is he happy? Does he have a message for me, for my family?"

"He wants you to know that he is happy. He did not suffer when he died."

Thank God. My mother always worried about the fact that he might have suffered. I will have to tell her this.

She continues, "He wants you to know that you are not alone. He is always watching over you, all of you, and helping to guide you in the right direction. If you need guidance, just ask him."

Yes, I have been doing this. I'm so relieved!

Before I can ask him anything else, she says he is gone; someone else needs to speak with me. Someone else? He is *the* person I want to speak with right now.

"He is his father," she says.

"Whose father?" I ask.

"His father, he wrote his son a letter..." she replies.

This can only mean be one person: it's his father. He wrote him a very hurtful letter. He had shown it to me, and I was shocked by the words. I told him to rip it up, to throw it away. I told him, I'm sure your father forgives you. Let it go. But he couldn't bring himself to do it.

She continues, "He wants his son to know that he is sorry and that he forgives him. He says, 'Get rid of the letter. Rip it, burn it, just get rid of it.'"

I pause for a minute. Wow. I'm floored. I knew I was right; his father didn't mean what he said. People often regret things they say and do. And forgiveness is important. I know I have to tell him this. But would he believe me? *I'll worry about that later.*

"OK, he is gone," she says and shifts in her chair. "There is a woman, an older woman, with wavy, short hair. She is small and frail looking, but she is actually spry and vibrant. Very strong woman. She also is speaking with an accent," she finishes.

I think for a minute, not knowing who this person could be. *Oh!* I suddenly realize it's my stepfather's mother. An amazing woman who at the age of 70-something once went up on our roof in the middle of a storm when she was visiting to clean the gutters.

I'm surprised because, while we had spent some time together and I loved her dearly, I never felt I connected with her at a deep enough level for her to appear during the session.

The medium continues, "This woman has a gift for you. It's a rose."

A rose. I sit there, open-mouthed, because two nights ago, I had a powerful dream. In this dream, I was given a necklace, an intricate design with a rose at the center. I even drew pictures of the rose in my journal. The rose seemed important, although, like always, I had no idea why. Finally, an answer!

"This person is presenting you with a rose. A red rose," the medium continued. "And a message. Every rose has its thorns— the more beautiful the rose, the more painful the thorns," she spoke.

The first thing that pops into my head is the Poison song. What she tells me is a bit different. Yes, I understand the meaning. This whole situation with him, the love, the heartbreak, the difficulties. He is the rose. I am the rose. *We* are the rose. This connection is the most beautiful rose I have ever encountered. And also the most painful.

She adds one more thing: "The rose is there; it is your decision whether to pick it up or walk around it."

I want to pick it up, I think, despite the pain it has brought and will very likely bring. In my mind it is positively worth it. More than worth it. The rose is love. My soulmate. I decide right there, I will pick up the rose and experience whatever comes.

I want to ask one last question, because it seems to me that even if I pick up the rose, everything is out of my control, and it is really up to him to make his way back to me.

"What do I do?" I ask.

The answer:

Just be.

Damn, the hardest thing for me to do. I want to be able to do something, take action, fix it all... This will be difficult, but I need to trust.

DECEMBER HOPE

t is late December, one week before Christmas. I am on my way to meet him for a drink. It has only been about six weeks since we saw each other, although it feels far longer. I reached out to him on Thanksgiving, wishing him a happy holiday, telling myself that I had no underlying intentions behind the text. I missed him, it was a holiday, and I wanted to see how he was. He was the one that suggested we get together and I said yes. I wanted to see him, and who knows? Maybe he had changed.

I am excited, but nervous. I had a dream that I met him and wore my orange dress, so that's what I'm wearing today. I feel confident. I have a lot to share with him, especially my metaphysical experiences over the last several weeks. Will he believe me? For some reason, I think he will. I feel like I am *supposed* to tell him. Mostly, though, I want to prove to him, and to myself, that I am fine, balanced, and have moved on. Am I hoping for a reunion? In all honesty, yes. But I also know that if it doesn't happen, I will be OK. I keep telling myself I am balanced, I am happy, I am free. I am here just to talk, we are friends, there is nothing romantic.

I park and realize I'm more nervous than I thought. I am actually shaking. I take a few deep breaths, semi-meditation, and I soon calm down. A little.

I walk in, and there he is at the bar. I see him before he sees me. *OK, here I go.* He turns, sees me, and smiles. That smile. I had really missed him. And I still want him. *I have to be in control, be cool, act like it's not a big deal to see him.*

We flow easily into conversation, catching up on families, activities, and work. I had decided before the meeting that I was going to tell him about all of my recent experiences—the synchronicities and my spiritual awakening—but now I'm not sure where to begin. Will he believe me, or will he think I'm crazy? I've only told two close friends and some supportive family members about this, but they are believers. I decide to just speak. I have nothing to lose, and I'm tired of holding everything inside.

So, I just casually tell him. My dreams, visions, how I had run into the one-eyed man in real life. *What a shocking experience that was!* My numbers... He asks a lot of questions, genuinely interested.

"Do you believe me?" I ask.

"Of course. I believe in a lot of things," he replies.

I'm relieved. He doesn't think I'm crazy.

We laugh because the woman sitting next to us is obviously eavesdropping on our conversation.

"Excuse me, but is there anything else you want to know?" he asks her, jokingly.

She smiles and ignores him and we both laugh. He touches my knee. Nothing obvious, just a friendly gesture. I try to ignore it. I'm telling him about my Reiki, and I gently touch his hand, emphasizing a point. *Also a friendly gesture,* I think to myself.

I'm definitely feeling tipsy. It seems to happen in slow motion. We move toward each other, nobody taking the lead, and we kiss...well. One thing leads to another, as they say.

I wake up and look at him. I'm trying to sense what he is feeling. Nothing. It had been an incredible night. He shared some old pictures with me. Man, he was good looking. Not that he isn't now, but I loved seeing him in his younger days. And he shared some stories from his life. He was very open. I'm tired. I might have only slept two hours, at most. But it was worth it. I was really happy to be with him here, right now. No negative vibes, no fears. I feel confident and strangely powerful. I am fearless.

However, he wakes up and there it is—the distance. I'm actually a bit surprised, even though I know it shouldn't be surprising; after all, this has happened so many times in the past. But it doesn't bother me as much as before.

"So," I ask him. "Where do we go from here?"

No fear, I am feeling no fear about saying what I want, speaking my truth.

"Well, let's see how things go. But I think we should see other people," he replies, without looking at me.

I freeze for a moment. Think for a moment. I'm shocked and hurt, but I remain calm.

"OK," I reply.

I have to leave. I can't stay here feeling like this. I need to get home.

"Oh! I have to go. I'm late." I decline coffee, kiss him goodbye, and speed home.

My mind is racing. What the hell just happened? I should not have slept with him. I feel like last night was out of my control. Yes, I made the decision to sleep with him, but it wasn't a smart decision, not one I would normally make. I think. *Dammit.* What is normal? I should have been more careful. My thoughts are all over the place. Did I make a mistake? I feel yes, because I am feeling the attachment again, my desire for him increasing even as I try to push it away. Swallow, swallow, swallow—no success. *What's the big deal?* I could still see him; we would just be seeing other people. *But I can't! I can't do this.* I need all of his attention and I don't want to share him. It's the way I am. However, I had just agreed to continue to see him and date other people. Or more likely, see him while *he* dates other people. I'm not interested in dating anyone else. Shit. I don't want to do this. This will not work. *I want more than that.*

I text him as soon as I get home. I want to get clarification. Or maybe I'm just hoping he's changed his mind.

Me: Hi. Thanks again for last night. Just wanted to clarify, we are dating other people?

I sound like an idiot. I'm sure he knows what I'm doing.

Him: Yes.

Me: OK, I don't think I can do this. I'm not good at sharing. This will be too hard for me, so best that we don't see each other. Good luck to you.

Him: OK. I get it. I wish you the best.

That's it. I wait for another text from him, but nothing comes.

Why did I just do this? Even if I think I can't share, maybe I can. I am confident enough and maybe I should have tried. No, I want all or nothing. I want him desperately, but I also know eventually I would grow insecure and jealous. The old me might have agreed to this arrangement. *I know my value and I know what I want.* I actually feel more confident, saying these words to myself. I'm not just someone that he can reject whenever he's afraid. I'm done; this time I'm really finished with him. I will move forward, live my life, meet someone new. This is the new me. I am walking away.

Damn, I was so caught up in the throes of passion, I realize I forgot to tell him about his father. Another time? Or maybe it's just best to let it be.

Winter comes, craziness of the holidays. I'm not happy, but I'm also not devastated. I still think about him, but keep myself busy and push the thoughts of him aside when they try to creep in. I'm trying to figure out my own life. I need to find work, something I am passionate about, but I have no idea what I want to do. I don't feel pressured though. I feel like I have time, and something will come to me eventually. I'm patient.

December 15, 2018, 8:22 p.m., the date of my mysterious numbers, comes and goes. I sat and waited for something to happen. I paid attention, listened for messages, watched the news. It was just an ordinary day. At least I know now that the numbers do not correspond to that date, at least nothing openly. *Oh well.* Back to the solving the puzzle.

I can't believe how much information I've written in my journal. And most of it makes zero sense. I want to know what everything means. I try to remember the words of the medium: just be. So I am patient.

I start dating again, unenthusiastically. But I force myself to go out and meet men. I hate online dating. Ugh. But I go. I do meet a couple of men that show promise and I am interested in them, but they disappear. Poof. Gone. I feel like I'm losing my confidence. I never had this problem before. Usually I am pursued. I don't think I've ever really chased anyone, except for him. I definitely chased him. And now, it seems, I'm only connecting with men who don't want to pursue me. What are they afraid of? Because I do sense fear when I read them. Are they afraid of me? I wonder if there is something wrong with me. Am I broken now, because of him? I have no idea. I'm frustrated and tired of men, and I can't understand why nothing is working out for me. I think I'm a great catch. But why aren't any good men fishing?

I really start to miss him mid-winter, during the cold, dark days of early February. I repeatedly ask the universe for signs. *Universe, please send me a sign. Should I reach out to him?* I've cut myself off from his emotions. I purposefully avoid reading him from a distance. It's too overwhelming. So I sit tight, impatiently waiting for a sign. I'm not sure what the sign will mean, but I will figure that out when the time comes.

One night I have a dream. The hawk from my earlier dream is kiting above me, in large, swooping circles. His pattern changes and he flies in a figure-eight shape, leaving a trail of gold, a luminescent golden infinity symbol. Then the gold falls from the sky, covering me in shimmery dust. It's a powerful dream, and I wake up trying to piece the meaning together. I make my coffee and head out to the deck to do some research on hawks. It's the middle of winter, but on sunny days I have my coffee on the deck. I'm sitting in my parka, enjoying my coffee, when I see two hawks almost at eye level, kiting. Of course, I connect them to my dream. I was just dreaming about a hawk. *I know it's a sign.* But what does it mean? I sit quietly for a moment. It must mean that it's time. It's time for us to reconnect. So I text him.

DON'T BE
A STRANGER

My text, of course, led to his invitation to get together, just like last time. I need closure. There were many things that still were left unsaid, many questions unasked. I want to tell him what I'd learned, especially about why I feel so bound to him. Most importantly, I need to tell him about the message from his father. Of course, I also just want to see him. Maybe one last time, a final goodbye? Or maybe he will be ready this time? A false hope, I know that. I also sense that he needs to tell me something. There is something important that he hasn't told me yet and he will tell me today. I'm not entirely sure I'm going to like what I'm going to hear. I'm pretty sure that was confirmed earlier today when a bird sat on my deck and screeched at me for two minutes. A warning. I am prepared.

We meet at the same place, this time getting a table because of the noise at the bar. We catch up, our usual, very comfortable, casual conversation. Like before, effortless. We were always able to reconnect quickly. I'm eager to tell him about my spiritual adventures. He's telling me a funny story about something at work and my mind starts to wander down the path of incessant thoughts about him and our future. Of course, this leads to emotional disarray.

I had promised myself I would remain in control and I felt confident I would do so...but now, I feel that old familiar sadness come over me. The feeling of loss, the dark feelings from the past. I can't imagine why this is happening. I had arrived at such a positive place, after months of self-healing, and cutting the cord that tied us together. *And now, I sit here feeling bound again.*

I try to shake it—I flash him my positive, everything-is-perfect-in-the-world smile. It's time. I tell him about my Reiki classes, mediumship practice, reading tarot cards. I have my journal with me; I impulsively grabbed it on my way out the door. I open it and read some of the entries that still confuse me. As I speak, I can tell he is shocked. Does he recognize these things? He says yes. Some of these visions are memories from his childhood. I'm impressed, but not too surprised. I knew these images belonged to him.

I finally ease in and tell him about the medium. I said she had a message from his father.

"Do you want to know what it is?" I ask.

He stares at me stone-faced. I can read him very clearly. He is angry.

"No," he says. "No, I don't want to hear it."

"Are you sure?" I ask. "I am supposed to tell you this, and you need to hear it," I tell him.

"No, I don't want to ever hear it."

His anger comes through in his words this time. I realize, I have never actually seen him angry. I don't push it any further. I'm disappointed and return my journal to my purse.

There is something else, I think to myself. *He wants to tell me something.* I ask him point blank if there is anything he wants to tell me, something I should know.

"I've always felt there was some secret that you're hiding from me," I say, carefully. "Is there some deep, dark secret I should know about?" I smile this time, trying to keep things light.

There is something more behind the excuse for the walls. I know it. In the past, I wouldn't have asked. But today, I am different. I'm confident and not afraid of speaking my mind. Not afraid of judgment, criticism, or conflict.

He takes a deep breath. I can tell this is difficult for him.

"A few months before I met you, I had just ended a relationship. I loved her, and she wanted to get married. I didn't. So she broke it off." He pauses.

I'm staring at him. I finally learn the truth, and it's not at all what I expect. I continue to listen, shocked; I expected to hear something from his long-ago past, some deep, dark secret that formed the man he is now.

"I thought she was my soulmate and it destroyed me. I was a mess for a very long time." He stops talking.

I can't believe what I am hearing. I listened to a story of a broken relationship, his own heartbreak and devastation. He suffered through a difficult breakup, less than a year before we met last fall. She was his soulmate. I am upset, although I didn't let him know. I nod understandingly.

"I'm so sorry to hear about that," I reply, unsure of what to say next.

Why was he heartbroken...I thought he had walls? Did he let down those walls for her and then put them back up with me for self-protection? Is he actually capable of love? Is he capable, but not with me, because he is still recovering? Or is it just because it's me? Yes, my mind starts spinning out of control, after months of peace and silence.

I understand his fear of feeling pain again. I feel his fear. He doesn't trust himself. He is so afraid. I feel the fear as if it were my own; I feel the pain right in my own heart. I want to comfort him because I truly understand his pain, but I am so upset. *He doesn't deserve my comfort.*

I want to ask him all the questions zooming through my mind, but I stay silent. *He still loves her.* A great sadness overtakes me. He had told me before he had never been in love. And I believed him. It was a lie. This is difficult to hear and accept. Since we have known each other, through everything, he had adamantly told me that he had never been in love, never loved anyone. This, this harsh and shocking truth, is deeply painful. Why can't he love me? How can he love her but not me? *I just want to leave.*

This new knowledge makes a lot more sense. *The walls are there because he is afraid of feeling pain, loss, heartbreak.* And he wants her back? I don't quite sense anything. *Are his walls up?* Does he want her back? I don't ask. I decide I don't want to know.

"I love you," I say confidently and matter-of-factly. "I love you unconditionally."

He flinches. I can tell he is surprised by my words. I'm equally surprised, because I didn't realize my love for him was unconditional until I said the words.

I continue, calmly and without fear, "It doesn't matter if we ever see each other again. I will love you always. We will always be connected, and I will always remember you." I smile. I am released. Finally.

I'm feeling very brave.

I ask him, "Do you think there's any possibility for us, that you could love me?"

I say this as casually as possible; I don't want to freak him out.

He immediately and adamantly says, "*Never.* We will never be together. I will never love you. My walls are never coming down. I built them on purpose; they weren't put up unconsciously. I want them up. And I will never take them down."

His voice and the resoluteness of his words fill me with bitterness and sorrow. But I sit there, stone cold, not expressing anything.

"Perhaps in another life, another future, or another universe, we are or will be together," he continues. "I know we have a connection—I feel it too—but we will never be more than this, friends, in this lifetime."

Watch out—I want to tell him but don't—*never say never. The universe has a funny way of forcing you to face those things you adamantly deny will ever happen.* He had just set himself up for change, for those fucking walls to come crashing down. Surrender is always better in the long run. The crashing tower is a far more painful way to get on the right path. He has to learn on his own, unfortunately, so nothing I can say will make a difference. I wouldn't want to wish the tower on anyone.

Hearing all of this, I'm shocked and devastated. My throat feels tight; something needs to be released. *I'm not crying.* Whether the universe responds to his adamant disavowal of love does not mean we will be together. It could be anyone else in his future, the beneficiary of the destruction of the walls. I cannot foresee those walls coming down anytime soon though. That would require copious amounts of divine intervention. We all have free will, but sometimes you have to surrender. But some are not willing to surrender. He is one of those. The universe could guide him toward a certain path, but the decision whether to take the path, that is all his. I wonder if the universe keeps trying, even after people refuse to follow their guidance. Would he eventually realize that he should follow a path to love? Perhaps with me? No. I know he will not opt for a romantic relationship with me. Not now. Quite possibly, not ever.

As these thoughts run through my head, I am overwhelmed. I lose control and tears well up in my eyes. *Stop it*, I tell myself. I need to leave. I get up and tell him I need to leave. I do not want a repeat emotional breakdown.

"Please stay," he asks.

So I stay, even though I really just want to get the hell out of there. We talk a bit more about trivial things, but things grow silent. I don't want to be here anymore, and I feel he is ready to leave too. We call it a night.

He walks me to my car, being the gentleman that he is, and we say goodbye. He hugs me as I stand stiffly, still trying to figure out what this all means, this night. I know this is probably the last time I will see him, and this provided the closure that I need to move forward. But I am dying inside. He turns to walk to his car, as I stare at his back, feeling a tremendous loss.

He turns around and says, "Don't be a stranger."

Go to hell, I say to myself. *Don't be a stranger? What am I, your best bud?*

"You too," I scoff. I continue watching him until he gets in his car. I finally get into my car and drive away from him as fast as I can.

I cry like a blithering idiot all the way home. Not just tears, but huge sobs, releasing the pain, the loss, the betrayal, and the anger. Not only at him, but at the universe for making me think we would end up happily ever after. All the signs had pointed to him. Always. But somehow, I must have mixed up the message. I feel foolish and used. He has broken my heart yet again. I am finished. Even if we are meant to be together, supposed to be together, I am done with him.

HERMIT MODE

I clearly remember the drive home after we said goodbye. The finality of it—the pain, the darkness (ah, my old friend!)—I thought I had already expunged all of these emotions from my system. I keep replaying that goodbye in my mind. Watching him walk away and he turns around, with a casual, "Don't be a stranger." After all we had been through, after all the meaningful conversations, vulnerable discussions, he had the gall to say those words to me. I never felt that this was a singular journey. I feel we were both part of this together. Maybe I'm wrong. Maybe this is not about *us*, but about *me*.

"Goodbye," I say aloud.

I consume myself with learning about spiritual healing. I take another energy healing course. I learn to read tarot cards. I have many vivid and powerful dreams to analyze. I'm not lonely and I don't miss him at all. In fact, I feel like I'm finally free from his energy. I imagined cutting the cord between us several times, and it worked. I don't want to be connected to him anymore. I do my best to work on myself, instantly cutting off any thoughts that come into my head about him. It helps to have another distraction too. I'm casually dating, not really wanting anything serious. I am happier.

So many dreams, so many meanings. My impatience to have everything happen quickly, my desire to find my happily ever after, sends me into a whirlwind of crash courses in self-improvement, Reiki sessions every week, several daily meditations, writing, dating several times a week, friends, family, and praying for the universe to please hurry up with my healing... I need to slow down. I am moving at breakneck speed and my journal is completely full. I need a break.

DEEP BREATHING

I decide to take a break from the inner work. I still meditate and practice Reiki, but I stop trying to feel intensely connected to the spirit world. I need a break. I stop going with the flow and trusting the universe. I have full control of my life again and I'm not going to fall for false visions and imagine synchronicities in coincidental events. Maybe I imagined everything. Maybe those things I felt were because I wanted him so badly. I believed everything was telling me yes, you are meant to be together. I'm angry too. I feel deceived by the universe. I had been led on a path, very clearly in fact, and all I found was more pain, when I had expected so much joy.

Yes, I still believe in something bigger than myself, but I'm not going to follow any mission, plan, or crazy timeline because the universe is telling me to. Why would the divine, who supposedly has my best interests at heart, keep leading me back to him, when clearly it was an impossibility? I had free will, so I exercised it. I am taking care of myself, my life. Sure, I still find synchronicities and occasionally write them down, but no longer with the intense obsessiveness that had overtaken me. Woman on a mission. The mission is not about him any longer—it is about me, becoming whole, healthy, happy, and moving on to better things. He is not my soulmate; I am not infinitely connected to him. I am *me*, alone, strong, powerful, and I am moving on.

In retrospect, I probably shouldn't have taken a break. The down time unbalanced me and brought me back to thoughts of him. I tried to continue dating, went out a few times with men with some potential, but really, I had little interest. I made the decision that I would only go out with people that were very special and unique. I'd be particular, take my time. I was not in a rush to get back into anything serious. I was fine, even if still partially heartbroken. Heart-cracked. Slowly, the pain was easing.

In late summer, I wake up in a cold sweat from a very disturbing dream. A nasty, devilish creature captured me. I felt his rage and hatred as he grabbed my wrists and held me down. I was terrified and struggled to escape. Suddenly he appeared, my soulmate, my lover, the man I vowed to forget. I screamed for him to help me, help me get free from the devil. But he faded away—whether by choice or not, he disappeared, as I continued to plead for his help. I was, however, finally able to escape from this dark devil on my own.

Why didn't he help me? Why didn't he free me from the devil? I rationalize: this dream represents my need for him and his inability to give me the love that I want. I'm fearful that I will be trapped, forever bound to him. I am helpless and I think that only he can save me. I had presumed that only his love could set me free. In reality, I was able to set *myself* free. This whole situation, our toxic relationship, is my own doing and I was the one that needed to take action. He was and would continually remain stuck. If I want change, I need do it alone. I don't need him to fix things.

It's four a.m. I need more sleep. I fall quickly into another dream. I am climbing a tall, steep mountain, ascending through the clouds. I am buried several times, covered in rocks and dirt, but I manage to dig my way out, clawing my way through with my bare hands. It's a difficult climb. But I manage to reach the top, triumphant. I felt like I had conquered something, maybe my fears, maybe my insecurities. I am filled with hope.

I'm not sure what prompted me to reach out to him in late August. My dreams? Perhaps my feeling of prevailing peace? My need to let this not end in anger? Or were these all excuses? Whatever my reasons, I texted him, just a hello, checking in, asking how he was doing. As per the usual past patterns, my hello turned into setting a time to see each other, per his suggestion. Again, I'm sure deep down that's what I wanted, but when I first sent the text, that was not my outward intention.

What am I trying to accomplish? What is my goal? Closure? Don't I already have closure? Honestly, I felt it was something I had to do, to see him again. The only difference was that this time, I had no expectations at all. I did not expect anything from him except friendship. I was just going with the flow again, trusting that there was something I needed to learn from the meeting.

He suggested the same place we had met before. I was uncomfortable about that.

"We have such great memories there, are you sure?" I joked.

We agreed on a date and time. However, I looked at my calendar and realized that I had a first date with someone, on that same exact date and time *and* place. I thought that was a little synchronistic. So I cancelled my date with this stranger. Wasn't interested anyway.

Of course, I thought seeing him might be a mistake. I went through every possible scenario and imagined several different outcomes. What was I expecting? I did not expect for him to open his heart to me. I didn't expect a reconciliation. Just a reconnection and possibly friendship. I was thinking very logically and clearly. Intuitively, I felt only positivity. Nothing negative was coming through. I decided it was going to be OK. I was much stronger now and I saw the bond between us as just a strong, non-romantic connection.

Funny, I wasn't nervous at all on my way to meet him. Not like the other times we met. I felt like I was on a purposeful mission, although the mission itself was unclear.

I arrive, and he is already at a table. I walk up to him and we hug, and, like always, the quick catch-up. Already I feel this meeting is entirely different. I feel in control, clear. I feel powerful, but not in a victorious and selfish way. I feel a power within that gives me the ability to speak my truth without fear. I like this new me.

He tells me he is seeing someone, but he isn't sure about her. Surprisingly, I'm not jealous. He says he has been trying to break up with her for a while, but she keeps coming back. *Hmmm, sounds familiar.* He is feeling stuck about what to do. *I feel like I'm having deja vu.*

"She isn't even that attractive, and the sex is not that great," he says. "Unlike with us..." He smiles.

I don't reply to that. No way. I think to myself, *He is doing the same thing to her that he did to me. Keeping her hanging on a thread, the whole back and forth...* I know it's different because I scare the shit out him. But still, his fear of intimate commitment is pretty obvious.

"Why don't you just break up with her?" I ask pointedly.

He shrugs his shoulders. "I don't know."

We are talking open and comfortably, like friends. Good. I want friendship.

"I want to feel your energy," he says. I had just finished telling him about the heat I feel in my hands when I am performing Reiki.

I hold his hand and close my eyes...and he kisses me. Damn. Damn. Damn. And, what's worse, I kiss him back. I did not expect this at all. If I had, I would have figured out a way to get out of this situation ahead of time. However, I remind myself that I am in control. I decide to go with the flow...still...we sit and talk for a while longer, continuing to hold hands.

He asks for a ride home, since he had walked to meet me. Sure, I don't see any problem with that. *Yes, of course I have a problem with that!* I remind myself to just drop him off and leave. *Do not get out of the car. Do not go in his apartment.* As we say goodbye, we kiss again, more deeply this time, and he asks me to come in.

"No, not a good idea," I reply, adamantly. I really want him, but I know how it will turn out. "We will both regret it. I know exactly what will happen. I will wake up tomorrow feeling attached and you will run away as quickly as possible. Definitely not good."

He is quiet for a minute. "OK. I know, I know."

"OK, I guess I should go. Thanks for dinner," I say.

As he opens the door to get out, I ask, "How about we get together this weekend instead?"

"Sure," he smiles.

He kisses me again, then leaves.

"I'll text you," I tell him, as I drive away.

I text him a couple of days later. He says he's busy, but maybe tomorrow. I try one more time, and, again, I get the brush off—busy and no explanation. Here we go again. He is perpetually stuck and cannot move forward in any way with me, ever. Nothing new. I decide to let it go. I don't see any point in having any kind of relationship with him, including friendship.

My phone buzzes. It's two a.m. It's him, asking me if I want to come over and get drunk. *What?* He must be drunk. I knew all he wanted was sex. I ignore the text and reply after I have my coffee the next morning.

Me: I was sound asleep when you texted and it's a little too early now to get drunk :)

Him: :)

I'm angry.

Me: Why did you text me at two a.m. to get drunk, ha ha

I knew exactly why he texted me, but I want to hear him say it.

Him: It was a booty call :)

My anger turns to fury.

Me: I don't appreciate being treated that way nor being thought of as nothing more than a booty call. Don't contact me again if that's the only way you see me.

I have never spoken to him that way before; I have never been that angry with him before either.

Him: I'm so sorry. I really am. It won't happen again.

I could sense he was genuinely sorry.

Him: You're just so damn irresistible I can't control myself.

Great. It's always flattering to hear that someone finds you irresistible, but it's not what I want to hear right now.

Me: That's a problem. We have this deep connection and attraction, how can we be friends?

By the end of the conversation, he agrees that we can't be friends, and we decide no more contact. Ever. We go our separate ways and neither of us will reach out again. Goodbye. Again.

There is nothing more I can do. There is part of me that wants to help him. I am a healer, after all. But people need to want to help themselves, and true healing can only start once you have the courage to heal. He is stuck. I only hope he will be free one day and finally find happiness.

THE TOP
OF THE MOUNTAIN

The best view comes after the hardest climb.
~ Unknown

am at peace. I feel emotionally balanced, spiritually centered, and full of gratitude for my experiences over the last year. I start organizing my book. All the pieces are scattered all over my computer: books that I started but did not complete, various short stories, and, of course, my journal. I haven't done much writing in my journal lately. I haven't felt the need. Even when I see signs or synchronicities, I recognize the important ones and I remember them.

Who would have known one simple action would finally release me? After we decided no further contact, I still didn't feel like I had closure. I felt there was still something that needed to be done. There was unfinished business.

I read everything I had written, hoping to find an answer to this mysterious sense of incompleteness. As I read through the journal and the notes on my computer, I found something I wrote several months back. It's a goodbye letter. *Wow. I wish I had said those things to him in person.* Those were words I should've told him a long time ago. There was so much risk telling him before, but I saw I had nothing to lose. *It's over between us; I'm no longer fearful to say what I think.*

In the letter, I wrote about my realization that my emotions prevented me from thinking clearly. His rejection and the loss made me unable to process logically. I couldn't see nor accept the whole truth—that he didn't love me. And I couldn't let go because I was fearful that this was my last and only chance at having a connection of such depth and beauty. I too was guilty of running away—several times I put an end to things, before he had the chance to reject me. Pre-emptive strike.

I texted him all of these thoughts, one very long and very detailed text. What was I accomplishing? Setting him free? Setting myself free? I don't know, but I knew it needed to be done. This was one of those intuitive moments that made little sense.

As soon as I pushed send, I felt absolute freedom. Closure. I no longer felt bound to him. I no longer sensed that this was meant to be...the knowing was gone. Completely. I'm not sure how one simple text changed everything for me, but it did. For the first time, since the first time we kissed, since that first night when I knew I loved him, I am free. Truly free.

With that freedom finally came clarity. This was never going to work. My hope was based on him changing. I wanted him to change so badly, I hoped he would awaken and tear down his walls. However, I realized what I had needed to do was accept that he could not love me, could not be in a relationship with me. Acceptance paves the way to moving on. Hoping for someone to change is unrealistic. I believed this for over a year. A whole damn year. Me. The woman who thought I would never be one of *those* women, waiting for a man to change. All because of a connection that I thought had to happen.

Release and acceptance. And finally, power; power over my emotions about him, I felt in my power. I'm not anxious anymore about his return. I know now that if he ever comes back, I will say no, even if he has healed and grown. My emotions will not overtake my clarity in thinking and I will feel calm and know what to do.

I didn't get a reply for a few weeks and when it came, it shocked the hell out of me. It was almost bizarre. It was like a stranger had texted me. When I first read it, my reaction was laughter. I laughed because of the absurdity of what he said. He basically said that we had broken up over a year ago and my "continued communication" made him uncomfortable. Further, he has been in a relationship with someone for the last several months. I laughed again. I remember clearly what he told me that night about his "relationship," how he complained about her and how he wanted to end it but couldn't. I wanted to ask if he told her how he wanted to sleep with me. I bet he didn't tell her that. I am so perplexed. He is either lying or he is actually still moving forward with someone that he was desperately trying to leave. I don't know. Nor do I care. I was just puzzled that he would say this to me.

"My continued communication." Well, I spoke my mind and, admittedly, some of it was brutally honest. I'm sure it shocked him. But it didn't matter. I was free. That's all I cared about. I didn't care what he thought.

My reply was short and sweet. "Fuck you" is what I wanted to say. *No, I can never say that, no matter what he has done. Be mature.* I was pissed, and still shocked by his words, after all we had been through. Instead I replied very calmly. I told him it's done. I released him and released the knowing as soon as I sent the text. I am free, moving on, and truly happy. I wished him well.

Damn it if he didn't text me back, not once, but twice and said, *Thank you, I hope you are truly happy* and the second time, maybe fifteen minutes later, *I hope you are truly doing well.* Why did he text this to me? My mind was racing in analysis mode. I tried to figure out what he meant by those words. Did he think I was lying about being truly happy? Did he mean it...did he really wish me well?

I think he was just trying to make himself feel better. Who knows? I realized his words didn't make a difference to me anymore. But I was still upset, because the tone of his initial text made it sound like I was pulling a *Fatal Attraction* scenario. Maybe he really did think that...I have no idea. I never pressured him in any way and I simply walked away when things didn't work, so I wasn't quite sure where that came from.

Do I think we will ever see each other again? I don't know, but I don't need to. I have no desire to get entangled with him again. I know now that whoever is meant for me will be a whole man: fearless, strong, and giving. I will meet him one day. I'm in no rush. I'm at peace and happy on my own. As I learn to live more authentically and live in the moment, I move closer to my vision of the future. This is a time for *me*. There is a new knowing. A knowing that I will achieve all of my dreams.

My memories of this year, the growth and learning, the light and darkness, the pain and love, all intermingled together to add to the story of who I am. A strong, powerful, confident, loving woman who is full of light and knows what she wants. I stand in my truth and in my power. I have climbed the damn mountain, which nearly destroyed me and buried me several times. I reach the top, in my brilliant orange dress, my hair flowing freely, a staff in my hand: The Empress. I plant my staff and look back at the winding path that brought me here and I can't believe I made it through the darkness.

And I know now I will not go back via the same path, but forge a new one, taking flight and soaring to new adventures. Free to be who I am, free to love how I want, free to land where I choose, and free to live the life I was meant to live.

So, thank you for rejecting me. Without that, I might never have even decided to climb the mountain and would have remained on the shore below, always wondering what was at the top.

LET IT GO

*In the end, only three things matter: how much you loved, how gently
you lived, and how gracefully you let go of things not meant for you.*
~ Buddha

*Sometimes letting things go is an act
of greater power then defending or hanging on.*
~ Eckhart Tolle

As I sit here in lockdown, the chaos and anxious uncertainty
of a global pandemic has filled our world. Death, fear,
sadness. It's hard to maintain my balance at moments and difficult
to be at peace. Yet, I finished this book during this time, having
the ability to look inward in the solace and putting the final pieces
of the story together.

Like Adam and Eve, I also started this journey with a certain
naiveté and emotional immaturity. Yes, I am a grown woman, but
when I met him, I really did become unhinged. I thought I could
change him. I saw his beautiful light beyond the walls. I had hope.
You see, there are two of them. The thoughtful, loving, and deeply
connected soul, and the other one: the cold, closed, running man.
I always hoped the two could merge and create balance.

Every decision I made, every choice, I had to make in order
to reach where I am right *now*. The most difficult journeys are

also the most rewarding. I picked up the rose. *I do not regret anything.* The pain was a necessary experience. It was my journey of healing and growth. And the journey continues. There is no end to either of those.

My search for answers became obsessive. I wanted the puzzle solved. I kept entwining myself with him, hoping to find what I was looking for. I finally understand. We cannot always know the why. We are not meant to. And just maybe, the answer will reveal itself to us at the right time. We cannot know our destiny; we can only try to make choices that align with our souls. We may hear the voice inside our head tell us to turn right, but we can choose to turn left. We have free will, and no future is set in stone.

If we pay attention, we can hear the guidance from within. Listen, then make your choice. I believe in everything. There are so many mysteries we don't understand, so many unknowns in our universe. They are at first discarded as "crazy" or impossible. Remember, we once thought the world was flat. What we don't know is probably a lot more than what we do know.

What do I expect now? What does the future hold? I'm moving forward one step at a time. Sometimes I don't know what awaits me on the next step; it's obscured in mist. Whatever lies ahead, I will find when I touch that next step. And I am comfortable with that. I trust that my choices will lead me to something beautiful. I have faith in the unknown future.

AUTHOR'S NOTE

always wanted to write a book, but I never believed I could actually do it. Sometimes you just have to take that leap of faith.

Some of you may ask: what is the truth? Did some of these events really happen? My answer is: the truth does not matter. It's all in how we experience our reality and what we create based on our understanding of events. I will say this: there was a woman, there was a man, there was an awakening, and there was a story. The two characters created their story long before they met in this life. Sharing their story was the final piece of the puzzle. Once the puzzle was solved, the journey was complete.

This marks both the end of an experience and the beginning of something new and exciting. I cannot wait to see what happens next.

On to the next tale. It's already germinating in my head.

Some final thoughts as you begin your new adventure:

Do not be afraid to take that leap of faith if your heart is telling you to. You will never know what beauty may come your way. Understand that we are all learning, and sometimes things do not turn out the way we planned. There are no mistakes, only choices that lead us to something new. Have faith in what you cannot see. What was once magic is now science. Create your own definition of magic. Be open to starting your own quest. Delve deeper, meditate, experiment. All of us have abilities and gifts we are unaware of; seek what it means to be spiritual and mindful. Know that the physical and material do not matter in the long run. The meaning of life is far deeper, and very individual. Surrender—don't try to control every aspect of your life. The best things happen when we least expect them. Reach out to the world from a place of love, not fear. If we act in love, we will receive love in return. Heal yourself. In order to find peace and live a fuller life, you must be open to healing. Transformation requires the desire and courage to heal. Most important of all, love yourself unconditionally. It is in this love that we are able to open our hearts to others and help them love themselves. We become the catalyst for change. I believe if more of us do this, we can have a significant impact on the darkness in our world. Imagine, a world of souls, full of positive energy, so powerful that even those who are trapped in darkness can emerge into the light.

Love and peace.

You have led the way and I have followed,
Obedient, observant, omnipotent.
My spirit saturated with loneliness.
The path has led me to a depth,
I cannot fathom. I am lost.
You brought me down to the dark,
Expecting me to rise up,
To fight for stability.
I didn't even recognize,
I am changed for the best,
When I felt changed for the worse.
Hope was once simply blind truth,
Now hope is uncertainty.
Sometimes knowing too much,
Is too much too know.
I would rather live oblivious,
To the future and what it will bring.
To enjoy the moments, to live,
Therein is the hope.
I chose hope and blissful ignorance.
And move forward to a life,
Unknown.
Only knowing there will be
Abundance and joy,
Balanced by pain and sorrow.
I believe in everything